OUR LADY OF THE PICKPOCKETS

Dilys Rose was born in 1954 in Glasgow.
After graduating from Edinburgh
University in 1974, she travelled widely,
beginning to write in 1980. She has
previously published two collections of
poetry, *Beauty is a Dangerous Thing* and
Madame Doubtfire's Dilemma. She lives
with her family in Edinburgh.

By the same author

DILYS ROSE

OUR LADY OF THE PICKPOCKETS

Minerva

A Minerva Paperback

OUR LADY OF THE PICKPOCKETS

First published in Great Britain 1989
by Martin Secker & Warburg Limited
This Minerva edition published 1990
by Mandarin Paperbacks
Michelin House, 81 Fulham Road, London SW3 6RB

Minerva is an imprint of the Octopus Publishing Group

Copyright © Dilys Rose 1989

The publisher acknowledges subsidy from the
Scottish Arts Council towards
the publication of this volume.

A CIP catalogue record for this title
is available from the British Library
ISBN 0 7493 9101 4

Printed and bound in Great Britain
by Cox and Wyman Ltd, Reading, Berks

ACKNOWLEDGEMENTS

The author would like to thank the Scottish Arts Council
for their support during the writing of this collection.

Grateful acknowledgement is also made to the following
publications where some of the stories first appeared:
*Glasgow Herald, Glasgow Magazine, I Can Sing, Dance,
Rollerskate* (Collins, 1988), *New Writing Scotland 6*
(Aberdeen University Press, 1988), *Original Prints 1*
(Polygon, 1986), *Original Prints 3* (Edinburgh University
Press, 1989), *Radical Scotland, Scottish Short Stories*
(Collins, 1986), *Snakes and Ladders* (Unwin Hyman, 1988).

Some of the stories have been broadcast
on BBC Radio 3 and BBC Radio 4.

FOR BRIAN

CONTENTS

OUR LADY OF

THE PICKPOCKETS

FOR MANY HOURS NOW NO BUSES have left. It is because of the rains. Everywhere is mud in my town, in Villa-hermosa. Her name mean 'beautiful' but she is not. Tonight she is a wet black sow and the tourists are stuck in her belly. My people know how to wait. Angél say they are all waiting, for death, or a Greyhound bus to Texas. It is all the same to them. Many times my people will wait all night in the bus station, without speaking, without moving. They know every way to sleep, up against the wall like sacks of beans, piled together on the bench, flat out on the floor. They sleep even with the eyes open. Angél say this is because they live with the eyes closed.

Tonight there is no sleeping on the floor. Sometimes Emilia, the desk-girl, she take her broom and sweep the water to the door. Each time she sweep, Owaldo check through the peanut shells and cigarette butts for coins. He find no coins, the black water always returns.

Tourists, they don't know how to wait: always they must be speaking or moving. They don't know how to do nothing. Each minute somebody get up and go look into the night. There is nothing to see but two or three

1

streetlights. Each streetlight has a cloud of mosquitoes in its halo. And under the mosquitoes, pariahs, always pariahs, pick-picking their sores. They are waiting, too, to die, or for something to die which they can eat.

In the bus station, nothing. In Brasil Street is a café-bar. It has tequila, beer and coffee but Emilia don't tell tourists a goddamn thing. She give them a rough deal. It is because they will not speak her language and she cannot speak theirs. Only money she knows. Dollars, cents, nickels, dimes. It is not enough. I know words. I don't have to spit-shine like Owaldo, day and night and no shoes on the feet.

'Madame,' I say, 'Madame?' This lady has hair like ripe maize. It swing over her face. She is drawing on a map, arrows. The arrows go up the page. They cross from one colour to another. The border is where the colour changes and at the border is a blue line, a river. Angél tell me about this river: American farmers shoot Mexicano wetbacks like rats.

'Madame,' I say. 'Where you go?' She look up at me so I smile. Angél say a smile goes a long way with gringos. Texas is a long way.

Madame sit beside a man who drum his boot heels on the floor. Madame put down her map on the bench. Beside her she has a backpack and a big skin bag. Beside the man is a backpack and a parcel.

'At least we got most of the stuff we wanted,' Mister say. He pat his parcel like pet. Madame has one arm inside her skin bag. She bring out cigarettes, cheap Mexican cigarettes. Angél smoke only American brands. She say, 'How long can we go on like this? One trip after another, one bus station after another. Can't we even get some wheels?' Mister twist round. He try to see Madame's face but it is hidden in the hair.

'We can't have everything,' he say in a quiet voice, a voice for a baby. 'You know that.'

'Everything! We can't have anything. After all this time we can't have what any peasant here can manage no sweat,' she say.

'Please Eleanor, I'm tired,' Mister say and turn away. Madame reach for her matches but they drop on the wet floor. I pick them up.

'Madame,' I say. 'Allow me.' I am always polite. You don't get nowhere but into the street without manners. I strike the match on my thumbnail. Angél he teach me this trick. Madame likes me now. It is enough.

Behind Mister's head I can see Angél. He is over in the corner pretending to read the newspaper but he is watching. Angél can read only photo-romances. Owaldo spit on Angél's boots. The boots must shine like hub-caps for Angél. It is normal.

'Madame, Texas?'

'San Cristóbal,' she say. Many many tourists go there, and to the ocean. Villahermosa has no ocean like Mérida, and no mountains like San Cristóbal, only rivers in the streets when it rains. San Cristóbal I have seen only in posters, since first I began sleeping here the same posters. On my first night, Angél he come up to me, he share my bench and share with me his blanket. He drink mescal and tell me about Texas. He say Villahermosa is a stinking pigsty. He say my eyes will fall out when I see Texas.

'After San Cristóbal, Madame, Texas?' She point to the

3

arrows on the map. Her finger with the sparkling rings it stop at every arrow – San Cristóbal, Oaxaca, Mexico City, Chihuahua, El Paso, Texas. A long way.

'No children,' I say. 'Madame, you, Mister, no children?'

'Not yet,' she say. 'But maybe . . .' Mister make a long face. He go look for the bus again. Madame she follow him with the eyes, the way pariahs follow the trash cart. Her eyes are hungry.

'No mother, Madame, no father. No home. Only the bus station. Only ten years old, Madame.' I am eleven but ten is a good number. Madame, she look at me for a long time like she trying to see under my skin. When she stop looking she give me chocolate. She believes. It is enough. I know how to wait.

Mister does not believe.

'What's your game?' he say. 'Here's a dollar. You get yourself off home.' He hold the note between his thumb and finger. His fist is tight. 'A real American dollar.' A dollar is not enough. 'Here, kid.' He waves the green paper at me. It is new and crisp. It crackles like pampas grass. I keep my hands behind my back.

'No game, Mister,' I say. 'No home. Take me with you, to San Cristóbal, to Texas. Please Mister?'

Mister turn to Madame. 'This is your doing, Eleanor,' he say. 'All this travelling's made you flip. Can't you even use some goddamn sense and say no? Jesus Eleanor, can't you manage more than *maybe*?'

For a long time they talk. I don't know all the words but I know what the voices say behind the words. Mister does not want to say yes to me. But also does not want Madame to be sad. One minute he say, 'Okay, if it's what

4

you *really* want.' And then, 'You must be outta your mind. You'll want to take along one of those scabby dogs next.' More talking and then she take his hand and whisper something. He laughs.

Everyone is picking up their bags and running to the door.

'Mister, Madame, the bus is here!'

I will ask about Texas tomorrow. Angél say one foot on the road can take you far. Everybody is happy now: I because I am on the road, Mister because he is holding Madame close, Madame because we are all together. She smile at Mister all the time until he fall asleep. While he sleep, she smoke. The lights in the bus are out and only an old woman is talking, to her chicken. All night I light Madame's cigarettes and watch her face glow in the flame. Like this, in the flame light, her face is like the Madonna in my locket. I wear the locket under my shirt. Angél stole it for me, from the stall of Our Lady, in the market. Our Lady of the Pickpockets. Tonight she bring me luck.

But this town we have come to is so small! There is not even a bus station. And cold! Madame say it is cold because we are above the clouds. So many mountains everywhere, nothing but mountains and chapels and low white houses. It is very early. The peasants are running down the mountains to market, bent under their loads. Very poor peasants – no mules. Madame, she think it is beautiful here but there is nothing for me. I don't want to carry bales of maize on my head until I die. Owaldo's father was a peasant. When he died, his back was bent like a meat-hook.

'Tomorrow, Madame, Texas?' I say.

'Cut it out, kid,' Mister say to me. Then to her, 'What about the sleeping arrangements? Have you figured that?' And she say, 'We'll work something out.'

Mister stop at a *hospedaje* on a back street. He go in and come back with the *señora* who is fat and ancient. We must follow her across the courtyard very very slowly, because she must rest on her stick after every step. It is a clean place, with flowers and fruit trees and tiles. A boy is polishing the tiles. Much work for the boy.

The *señora* give us a room. A room with two beds. For me alone, one bed! For this I thank Our Lady. Already Mister is taking off his clothes. Everything he take off, so slowly. He groan. He tug at his boots. He sound like he's sick but he want only Madame to stop unpacking and go to bed. He want to put his head on her chest and his hands . . . I know about these things.

'Sleep, sleep,' he call out like it's for sale. Madame close the blinds. The shutters are already shut but still the sun makes stripes on the walls, stripes across the big bed.

I take off only my shoes. Everybody is to sleep until noon. I am too hungry for sleep. Instead, I listen. Each sound I can hear, alone – the *señora* pounding *garbanzos*, the boy beating out a rug, the cart bumping over holes in the road. In Villahermosa, from first light, always I hear traffic and scraping and hammering from the new railway station. Maybe some day trains will run all the way to Texas, without stopping.

Inside I can hear the game in the big bed. It is normal. First whispers and bed-springs creaking. Now Mister's on top of Madame. It's begun. He put his head on her chest, he hold her down, hold on tight. It's like rodeo. Mister's a cowboy on a wild mare. Madame she buck but Mister hold on. He work hard not to fall off. He's breaking her in. There. He done it. He's won. Now he snore.

We have eaten a good meal and have been to the market where Mister buy twenty peasant dresses. He is happy because I save him much money. I bargain for him in Spanish. It is almost dark and we are walking through the crowds to the *fiesta*. Everyone in town must be going because the streets are packed with people. Madame hold my hand. Already she is being mother to me. I can hear noise all round – music from the shows and chapel bells and guns and rockets.

'We'll talk about it later,' Madame say.

'But Eleanor, we gotta take care of it tonight,' Mister say. Madame, she pretend she don't hear. Many times today it is like this.

'Eleanor,' he say. 'Look at me when I'm talking to you. What if we run into trouble? What if someone thinks we're trying to abduct the child?'

I do not know this word abduct.

We go round the shows. Mostly, I try a game and they watch. I win many prizes – cigarettes, glasses, toy animals, a key-ring. Madame buy me a bag for my prizes. Now the streets are crazy with noise. Drunk men are singing and dancing and the air smells of sausage and sweat and beer. It's like the smell of Angél's blanket, the one he share with me if I am good. Texas, Angél say, that's all you need to say.

'Mister,' I say. 'Tomorrow, Texas?' Mister is watching

the man swallow fire. I pull on his sleeve. He bend down so his face is next to mine.

'We've been through this before. Texas is not possible.'

'Possible, Mister, possible.'

'You like it here, don't you? It's a beautiful town. We're gonna try and fix you up here, with a priest maybe. You'll get a room maybe, all of your own. Believe me,' he say, 'Texas ain't so great.'

Angél is at the market. The rains have finished in Villahermosa and Emilia has washed the floor. Angél is selling my prizes. And Mister's watch and Madame's rings. I take them because they give me no money, not even when I say I go with them in the big bed. It is normal. But Madame cry and Mister yell,

'You see! Even he thinks that's why he's here. Everyone must think so. And you call him a child!'

Angél is happy to have the watch to sell and the rings. We will eat well tonight and the next night and the next. Angél say it is better to take your skin to the market, better to swallow fire, better to steal than to starve. I can use my eyes and my good smile and I have my Madonna. Now, under my shirt, I also keep Madame's map, with arrows going all the way to Texas. It is enough. I know how to wait.

MAYA

SHE CAME ON AT SOME NOTHING town where the bus stopped late in the evening, a dusty hot town where tired indifferent men sat and smoked bitter cigars, in the dull square, on cement benches, under a string of dim lamps, their feet dragging idly in the dark red earth, their faces in shadow. There was nothing to stop for there, except the use of an unlit stinking toilet in the roadside bar, or the purchase of a sticky *tamale*, a bottle of fizzy water. There was nothing of interest to the tourist. No ruins, no chapels, no ethnic markets. The scenery was flat scrub and there was nowhere much to stay.

But she had stopped there for an entire week.

'I like it here too much,' she said in her slow difficult English. She sat down after removing an embroidered rucksack from her back. Her face was flushed. She was sweating. She adjusted a spotted headscarf over straggly girlish braids.

She was travelling alone and so were you. To the same destination – Palenque – where you had both planned – for your own reasons – to witness the spectacle of Maya remains, immerse yourselves in the vibrations of another nation's history.

What were your reasons? Can you remember now as you sit in your newly-decorated flat, sifting through handfuls of old photos, deciding which to keep, which to throw out, which most closely match the memories you have preserved, though these, like the photos, are faded, ragged at the edges. Of that time, that place, that person.

Else was German, from a small town in the north which was, she said, a winter city, beautiful only under snow.

'I like the sun too much,' she said. 'Also the jungle. The Maya. Maybe together we go to the jungle, yes?'

'Yes. Maybe. Sure.' Anything was possible on your meandering itinerary. As the bus careered round bends in the road it was better not to see, you sat back, bracing yourself for bumps. You smoked cigarettes, Else hummed and nibbled on raisins. You conversed. Two among thousands, backpacking the gringo trail, two single women going solo – you had notes to compare.

'It is good sometimes to talk,' said Else. 'Better maybe than making love, *ja*?'

Your own contribution to the conversation: a string of tales of *en route* suitors who had sought consolation in your Northern features, the English language, an unprotesting body – on buses, trains, public benches, in stations, chapels, bars, museums, wherever tourists could be found, suitors whispering their loneliness into your ears, stroking you with their needy fingers, clinging to some morsel of romance before you dropped them off, one by one, at the first convenient junction.

Else listened a lot. Her concentration was visible. It was

hard work for her being confined to English. You knew no German so she had no choice. As the bus pulled into the station she said,

'I think we are making a different journey.'

'Have made,' you corrected her. 'We *have made* a different journey.'

'Ahh, my English is too bad, *ja*?'

At the *hospedaje* a double room was cheaper, so you took it. The town was pretty. There were some sights worth seeing. You'd stay a few days before embarking on the last stretch to Palenque. For your *pesos* you got two beds, two rugs on the floor, one table, one sink, a plaster cast of the Virgin Mary above one bed, a crucifix above the other. Else chose the Virgin Mary. It was all the same to you. The room was cheap, adequate, clean.

Else closed the shutters on the cool morning sunlight and quietly arranged some of her belongings on the table: some books, a child's teddy – old enough to date from her own childhood – an ugly little clay figurine, a bamboo flute. The things people travelled with. You travelled light. Everything was disposable. Else's books were not the kind to be traded for anything going in one's mother tongue. They were the solid, worthy variety. She held up one for your approval, an anthropology book about the Maya. This girl took her travelling seriously.

When you woke up, it was to the sound of Else vomiting into the sink. You rushed over with your towel and pressed it into her hands. This was the beginning of your respon-sibility; the offer of a towel, the only towel you possessed and now soiled with a stranger's vomit.

As soon as she recovered, Else flushed out the sink, rinsed the towel fastidiously, wringing it until her knuckles went white, twisting the cloth until it was tight and stiff as a rope.

You hadn't noticed but this wasn't surprising, considering all the layers of loose clothing she wore. You looked more closely then as she patted her stomach and smiled dreamily, giving the impression of being inside a bubble, a mystical bubble of expectation. But that kind of thing was outside your experience and you had every intention of keeping it there. To you, all she had was an inconvenient swelling which made her wear her patched jeans open at the waist and caused her to throw up.

In spite of her aura of spiritual well-being, Else still looked exhausted, though she had only just woken from a sound sleep. A bad sign. Travel could take its toll at the best of times, especially travel on the cheap, when an overnight bus ride or a few hour's kip on a bench often took the place of a good night's sleep. What was she thinking of, going on a trip of this kind, in *her* condition? Shouldn't she be resting up, feathering her nest, knitting bootees and matinée jackets? Shouldn't she be staying within reach of an antenatal clinic, instead of tramping through Central America with a rucksack on her back and a baby in her belly?

Not that you knew the first thing about pregnancy, having pushed the idea far into the unimaginable future. People with babies stayed at home and that wasn't for you. Not yet. People with babies dropped out of your life like unwanted baggage. You left them to get on with it.

That was what they wanted, wasn't it, to be left to roost under a cloud of talcum powder and nappies billowing in the wind like the sails of moored boats?

Not Else. She had taken the test, had her suspicions confirmed. She had given notice at the small knitwear factory where she worked, given notice at the house where she rented a small, cluttered room. She had withdrawn her savings of several years and packed her bag, filling up all the spare pockets with the decorative junk she couldn't bear to throw out. She carried her home on her back and – under her voluminous shirt – the biggest claim on her future.

'If I am well, baby is well,' she would say, and you couldn't deny that she looked after herself. She possessed an extensive collection of vitamins, minerals, herbal infusions. She dosed herself with these each morning, after the sickness had subsided. And after the medicine, the exercises.

Rather than hanging around while she went through the procedure with the squatting, the stretching, the deep breathing, you began to go out on your own, dressing in slim-fitting jeans and a skimpy T-shirt – you didn't want anyone to imagine that *you* were pregnant – arranging to meet up later at a small *cantina* in the plaza.

It was an easy-going place which offered value for money and an open outlook. The waiters took their time and expected their customers to do likewise. Three days running he had been there at a neighbouring table, sipping coffee and observing the activity in the plaza. Three sightings and you felt you knew him. He was different from the others, wasn't he? You could tell right away that he lacked the restless, anxious gestures of so many on the road, those who at X were already on their way to Y before heading for Z, those who clung to a route as if it were a safety line.

He had seemed pleased to be just where he was, comfortable. He sprawled on his hard little café chair as if it were a deep, luxurious sofa. When he offered to buy you a second cup of coffee you didn't refuse. In a comfortable, containable way he turned you on, this man who became your lover by lunchtime.

When Else arrived Paul was sitting at your table. As she began to warm to her favourite theme, your eyes were on him. The jungle. The Maya. The gist of Else's conversation was: how does one reach this tribe who continue to live as they have always done, without the invention of the wheel, without Christianity, contraception? You chipped in now and again with cracks about machetes and banditos. You let Paul know that you didn't share Else's pioneering spirit, her passion for the primitive. You let him know that you had passions of your own and agreed to meet him later that day, when Else usually took an afternoon nap. You did not consult her. She did not complain.

Else's English was bad but her Spanish was non-existent, so when Paul bid his calm *hasta la vista*, you ordered breakfast, as you had ordered every meal so far. When you and she had agreed to link up – only for as long as your routes coincided, without any commitment – it had been simply a practical arrangement, mutually suitable. You hadn't counted on becoming saddled with all these little responsibilities, like having to obtain not only your own requirements, but Else's as well. What had she done before she met you? How had she even obtained a meal, she who was so particular about anything she put in her stomach?

And she tired so easily. Your walks through the town were punctuated by her pauses. That day, the day you met Paul, she wanted to visit an obscure office where she thought she might pick up even more information on things Mayan. You would have suggested that she went alone but how would she have made herself understood?

The responsibility was beginning to chafe. You disliked the fuss, the effort involved in ordering complicated meals from simple kitchens, and standing at the roadside while Else took deep breaths and clutched at her still insignificant bump, and using up a morning combing mucky backstreets for an office that turned out to be shut.

Talking is better than making love, you had agreed. What did you talk about as you edged along the hot narrow streets, avoiding skinny dogs and handing over the occasional coin to children pestering for *pesos, pesos*?

You talked about Else's future. She was vague. What would she do for a place to stay?

'Maybe I am living in the country. Maybe I find a little house, grow some chickens.'

And the father?

'Maybe he make visit but I do not think. He likes too much the freedom. I understand.'

Else understood everything. She would not stay with friends or family in case the baby might spoil anyone's sleep other than her own.

And money?

'I am not needing too much money. I am baking the bread and growing the vegetable.'

Vegetable was a word Else never could pronounce and it made you laugh, as did the way she unwittingly dismissed the future in every sentence. Yes, you had some good times together.

When you met Paul during siesta time, when the sunlight was cruel, he took you to a cool, dark café in a deserted plaza. You spent the rest of the day with him. And the evening. And the night. Creeping into his tiny room in case the signora caught you and turfed you into the street crying *putana, putana* at your back. Whispering, smothering your laughter under his lumpy pillow, throwing off all the blankets, lighting the mosquito coil and watching it glow in the dark as you passed the tequila bottle from your mouth to his.

The next morning you hurried back to Else, full of apologies. She had waited in, expecting you to return in the evening. But she understood. You spent the morning running little errands for her, being more responsible than necessary – expeditions to the post office, the market, the chemist. She had been more sick than usual that morning. And she had fainted.

'I go blackout,' she told you, showing you the bruise where her head hit the sink. And you thought that if you had been there it might not have happened. But you couldn't watch over her every minute of the day. She wouldn't have allowed it.

As you dotted in and out of the room, dropping off her supplies, you noticed that she was unusually subdued. She was someone who liked always to be engaged in some activity wherever she was: in the room she embroidered, she ate, she studied her picture book, blew on her bamboo flute. The flute playing got to you at times as she only knew a couple of tunes right through and played them over and over. But that day, remember? She wasn't busy with anything.

'What shall we do today?' you asked, wanting to be obliging.

'Today,' she replied, 'I am resting.' She lay down under a pensive mother of God and closed her eyes. You showered, changed your clothes, went out in time to catch Paul in his usual seat at the *cantina*.

On Paul's bed that afternoon, you ate tacos and listened to the thunder, the rain lashing the streets and whipping up rivers of mud. And behind the storm, Paul's even-toned voice telling you – as you talked of Else and her plans, Else and her baby, Else and her bamboo flute – that you had a choice and sooner or later you would have to come to a decision.

Paul . . . there he is, standing next to Else. He is holding her dripping rucksack above his head, pretending to be Hercules. Now that's a photo which doesn't correspond with the memory, such as there is. One for the bucket. You've even forgotten his second name. He lasted no longer than any of the others. What grand schemes were laid, yet by the end of the journey north, neither of you could wait to part company. With Else it was different.

You didn't know how to leave her there, at the station, in the rain, an hour before the train was due. Nowhere to shelter, nothing to say, no way of making amends. You were ditching her in favour of Paul. You couldn't leave, not until Else insisted,

'You go now please. It is better.'

You scoop up the photos you've decided to keep, in the wooden cigar box, on the shelf alongside all the other decorative junk you can't seem to part with so easily nowadays. You are tired, nauseous. Inside you the baby twists and turns. It kicks. It flips about like a fish. You should put your feet up. Maybe take a look at that knitting pattern. At the clinic they told you to rest as much as possible.

That's the one you've been looking for . . . Else standing on the platform, twisting her braids, knotting them tightly around her head, ticket sticking out of a pocket, her huge anorak billowing in the wind. Was the train on time? Did she find the Maya? And later, a house in the country where she could raise chickens and bake bread? Else . . . her hair plaited like a harvest loaf, her arms folded across her belly, the darkness gathering around her, a squat figure on an empty wet platform.

You place the photo on the cluttered mantelpiece next to the keepsake she pressed into your hand as you left. You'd never liked the crude little figure, its featureless face, stumpy limbs, broad belly, but you'd hang on to it a while longer. It was, after all, a doll. The baby might like it.

LONDON

HE LEFT HOME WITH A SUITCASE containing two shirts, some underwear and a dozen rock'n'roll records. At six a.m. he arrived at the flat which his big sister shared with numerous students. He arrived with no plans and no money. At that time in the morning, she wasn't pleased to see him, and told him so, before she crawled over her snoring boyfriend and rolled off the mattress, the only real piece of furniture in the room. He looked out of the curtainless window while she wrapped herself in a bathtowel.

'You can't stay here,' she said. 'This is the first place they'll look.' She plucked a couple of cracked mugs from the stack of dishes in the sink aand rinsed them under the tap.

'I know,' he replied. 'I'm going to London.'

He drank his coffee in gulps, put the address and the five pound note she had given him into his pocket, and left. When he reached the A1 he stuck out his thumb.

He stayed with his big sister's friend – who didn't like rock'n'roll – for a week, listening to the gloomy songs she played incessantly, songs to kill yourself to. He didn't know what to say when his hostess unaccountably crumpled into a weeping heap. This happened several times a day. He made cups of coffee for her, changed the record when she felt too miserable to get out of her chair. He washed a few dishes and slept on the couch.

He stayed until two police officers arrived at the door. They escorted him to the station where they put him and his empty suitcase on a northbound train. He'd sold his records to help pay for his keep. His shirts had gone missing at the launderette.

On his return home, his mother was very upset about the shirts and his father was very upset about his mother being upset. Nobody asked him if he'd had a good time.

Some years later, on the rare occasion of a family gathering – in his big sister's plush new home – he is reminded of that episode in his life. It has never before been mentioned in the presence of his parents but now his sister, snug in a fluffy white armchair, is concentrating on the cockroaches, the suicide songs and the sour milk for breakfast. She is even reproaching herself for not having sent him home immediately. His mother is looking anxiously at his father who is looking at him.

'I had a great time,' he tells them. 'Wouldn't have missed a bit of it.'

NEW YORK

AND THE YELLOW CITY CAB DOESN'T even seem to stop, just slows down as it drops her off at the Majestic Hotel, just slows down long enough for her to jump out, her baggage wrapping itself around her legs like clingy kids. And the black cab-driver sneers at the tip she leaves on the pink, creased palm of his hand.

And inside, the desk clerk narrows his eyes and measures her up, as the sweat dribbles below the neckline of his greying vest, as he tosses her passport into the drawer and lets her crisp bills linger between his fingertips.

And she doesn't want the porter to carry her bags but he does anyway, leaving her free to take in the seediness of it all, the plastic columns and outsize plastic busts of Roman Emperors with which they've festooned the foyer. The strip lights only make things worse, illuminating the broken, the fake, the grimy.

And jet lag hits her as she follows the porter into the decrepit groaning elevator and along the eighth floor passageway with its matted carpet, spotted with burn holes and countless stains.

On into the room where the paint is predictably flaking

and nothing other than the most basic requirements are in evidence. Being America, this includes a television. It's on the floor by the window, half hidden by the curtain, like a neglected pet.

And the porter is waiting for a tip so she hands him some coins and locks him out.

Once inside, this room, the one she has looked forward to reaching for hours, which she has paid for in advance and chose for no other reason than the price, this room which she loathes and fears, makes her want to get outside, instantly.

For a moment she wishes she were back in Scotland, in that cold country cottage. There she could at least sleep. There she had done a lot of sleeping. There she had put aside every spare penny for her escape, put aside any expectations from life until her bags were well and truly packed, until her air ticket and travellers' cheques were purchased.

She'd trade in a minute that isolation for this. Skin-thin walls, the brittle snatches of conversation in languages she doesn't recognise filtering through, the stale odours – of unwashed bodies, cooking oil, cigars, gasoline – blown in by the air conditioner. And the window won't open. And looking out there are none of the famous sights of Manhattan, no glitz and shimmer, just a lightless shaft. At its pit, a heap of debris.

The hotel bar's the nearest place to outside she can face after so many hours of travelling. She's not ready for the unwelcoming streets where she has chosen to begin her adventure – poorly-lit slum tenements, the kind of thing common in cities at home, but bigger, hungrier. And after the tame domesticity of a year in the country, she's become slow, fearful of dark doorways on fast, dark streets.

And the bartender is hospitable, refills her glass – on the house – after he's queried her accent and she's told him she's from Scotland. And it turns out that he has Irish blood in his veins, which give him a connection, a line in conversation, gives her some consolation, although she's never crossed the short stretch of sea to Ireland. Instead, she has come all the way here.

She sits on the high, slippery bar-stool and watches the dark-haired young man polish the counter, bearing down on the smooth wood, massaging it with a firm even sweep. He wears formal bartender's dress and should look smart but doesn't, quite. More like someone hired at the last minute, just come in from the fields and dressed hurriedly for the job. But fields, there are no fields here for how many miles?

And she tries to imagine the city spanning out from the doorway of the long dim bar, the bar still empty. It's early evening. A few solitary customers have spread themselves out at regular intervals and the bartender keeps on the move, emptying ashtrays, washing glasses, mixing drinks with high-speed flair then resuming his polishing of the already gleaming counter.

And it's quite obvious by the time the music comes on and a small crowd has gathered, but he tells her anyway: Babe, I'm gonna have to neglect you. But if you need anything, yell. And don't let nobody bother you.

And she drifts into the rhythm of a jazz classic until she

is buttonholed by an elderly couple who station themselves in her patch of the bar.

By the end of the night she has made their acquaintance. New Yorkers all their lives, they find her terror of the streets just real cute. And she has to repeat everything she says, just so they can pick up on her weird vowels. She speaks to them for most of the evening. It seems the safest thing to do.

From drink to drink the bartender delivers a few more lines about his life. He wouldn't bartend for ever, he was setting something up and if she thought she might stick around a while he'd see her okay. Gotta green card, babe? he asks her, more than once.

And before they leave, the elderly couple offer her a free manicure if she cares to call into the 5th Avenue store where the woman has a nice little job. Also a guided tour of the city's nameplates from the man. We got so many famous people lived and died here, he tells her, it's unreal.

And her mind wanders into that unreal, unknown city, along famous streets, past famous landmarks, through famous people. It was all out there but so far all she had seen was the hotel foyer, elevator, bedroom, bathroom – with broken lock – and this bar.

And the bartender is pouring a large shot of whisky into a glass and setting it down beside her, even though he has covered the beer taps with cloths and turned down the lights and the musicians have already trailed their PA system across the floor and the remaining stragglers are putting their coats on.

And the only other place that she could go was back to

the room, with its creaks and smells, its bare bulb and the loneliness that would inevitably come on in such a place, so she stays where she is, sipping whisky long after the outside doors have been bolted. The only exit now is through the passage adjoining the hotel foyer. And the barman reminds her that being a resident, she can go on drinking as long as she likes.

And the barman tosses plans at her, plans to get her set up in a place he knows where they were always looking for foreign girls. And he reels off rates for this and that. And lies to tell when you go looking for work. And then the apartment. There's no way a girl doesn't need an apartment and he knows someone who lets apartments. And when he notices that she is no longer listening, that she's sliding down into the chair, drunk and exhausted, he pours her another whisky.

And when eventually she lurches to her feet, clutching her room key, he follows her, directing her to the elevator but she insists on climbing the stairs – all eight floors – hoping this might dissuade him. And his arms are supporting her because she can't walk straight and while they're supporting her he's mumbling into her ear something she can't quite catch. But she doesn't want to know what he's saying because there's no doubt now that he's hoping for something in return for the free drinks and he's bigger than her and it's late and she has no faith in the desk clerk helping her out as he's asleep in his booth. And she's in a foreign country and she feels so tired. She has the desire to push the bartender down the stairs and make a run for her door, but he's a stranger, and she's in a cheap hotel in New York. He might carry a gun. Didn't everyone, here?

He might be crazy. Wasn't everyone here? She doesn't want to die on her first night abroad.

And he's leaning hard against her as she turns her key in the lock, as she's extricating herself from his arms and wearily trying one excuse after another and none is having any effect. And the door is open and they can't go on talking in the corridor all night. It's already 3 a.m. and some people – even in this city which never closes – might want to sleep and their voices – hers wheedling, pleading, his forcefully friendly – are bound to disturb other residents.

And she doesn't imagine anyone would be too sympathetic to a drunken tourist who has picked up the hotel bartender.

And the door is closed with him on the inside.

And she still hasn't found a way of getting the message across.

And he is clumsily attempting to unbutton her shirt.

And she is thinking that this was not at all what she had planned for her first night in New York.

I CAN SING, DANCE,

ROLLERSKATE

COOL IN HERE. SO COOL AND dark. This has gotta be it. I'll say, You gotta real nice place here mister. Then I'll tell him. Why not? Hey mister, I'll say, I just walked all the way up 1st then all the way down 2nd, you know what it's like out there? I tell ya, it's hot. Not just regular hot but ninety-eight degrees hot, you hear me? Heard it on the radio five times already. Five times, after the same bit of news about today's shooting in Brooklyn and this month's TV star overdosing on vitamins, the weatherman broke in to give us an update on the temperature. It's murder out there, mister, folks riot in this kinda heat.

Sure I look wilted, but I'm all set. Even brought a spare outfit, in case you don't go for classic black. Some folks find black depressing, funereal, I know it, but it don't show the dirt.

You know what it's like out there? I'll say. It's like the desert. There's a haze, a shimmer over everything. The whole of Manhattan looks like it's underwater, like it's dissolving into the smog. You don't walk through that heat, mister, you wade through it, slow mister, real slow, like a dream sequence in a bad movie. Today's been one hell of a bad movie so far.

It's lonely out there, you know. Nobody's around. I mean nobody. The WALK DON'T WALK's been flashing off and on to no one but me. The whole goddamn city's deserted. But there's traffic, sure there's traffic, all heading the same way – outta town.

All the way up, all the way down for nothing, not even a maybe outta fifty establishments. More. More like a hundred. I'll say, You know how far that is, you ever tried walking it? No, you'd take a cab. All the billboards would slide by, red lights would turn green, the blocks would just melt away. You'd take a cab but I walked, mister, from 3rd to 88th, from 88th back to 3rd, that's 85 twice, 170 blocks – I can count good.

So maybe he heard the weather report already. So I'll tell him, Sure it ain't the best day for it but I don't have a choice, see. Okay, so nobody in their right mind hangs out in the city today if they can help it, but that's my point, mister, *if*. See, I just got here from . . . no, I live here, mister, sure I do. Just got back from . . . no, you won't know it. No sir, there's not a whole lot to know about where I got back from. So he wants to know where else I've worked in Manhattan. I'll say, Okay I'll tell ya. I'll make a list. I can count and I can lie.

Even without the heat, I'd still get the flushes, the dizzy spells, the throwing up. Your symptoms are quite normal, Mrs Lemme. Positive, *Mrs* Lemme. Acting like we're all married. Simplifies their filing system maybe. Ain't that good? she says. No kidding, I call on the phone at five after nine for the results and that's what she says. So I'm putting her straight, giving her some background when she cuts in with, We don't require any personal details, Mrs Lemme, meaning she don't want no sob stories or mess on her doorstep. A termination comes around three hundred, she says, snappy as ever, like it was a bargain offer. But you gotta go outta town. The inner city list is way too long for you, Mrs Lemme. You should have contacted us a month ago. And I just got here.

Twelve hours it took to get here on the bus, sitting way back by the stinking john, stuck between two slobs, one with a cigar on the go the whole way, the other with body odour. And the window jammed shut. Enough to make anyone sick. Twelve hours of going over potholes on the highway thinking, that one, that's done it. All it takes is a bump to get rid of it, a bump on the night bus. Some hope.

D'you wanna think about it? she says, meaning she ain't got all day to spend on me. Think about it? I ain't done nothing but. Watched all them women with kids go by past Marty's Grill, pushing their buggies up and down Main Street, piling groceries right in on top of their kids, hanging parcels on the handles of the carts. Every goddamn one of them run down, worn out, sick of their dribbling screaming toddlers. You bet I've thought about it. Toddlers are tough but that's just the beginning. Of the end. Sixteen years plus. That's one hell of a pile of tips. When d'you need the cash? I wanna know before she hangs up on me. In advance, she says. For sure.

What's keeping this guy? Don't tell me, I'll say, I don't look fit enough to fix a milkshake, right? It's the heat, I tell ya. Why not step outside, mister, see what I mean, sample that atmosphere. There's no one around, not even derelicts. Usually you're tripping over them, right? Usually they're like so many casualties strewn all over the sidewalk: guys with their legs in plaster, bag ladies with bandages instead of shoes, asleep or out of it. But not today. It's too hot even for them today. They've swarmed in Central Park. They're sprawling over a patch of shade. I don't blame them, mister. Just wait till you hear the news. There will be killings tonight.

So he wants to know why nobody hired me so far. Don't know what it was, I'll say, just bad luck, maybe. It happens. You'll know all about luck in the restaurant trade. Some days folks just don't wanna eat, right? Some days they only want what you just ran out of – you see, mister, I'll say, I'm familiar with the trade.

So he wants examples. No sweat. Take the seafood bar. I say to the guy, Okay so I ain't never boned a fish for a customer – most folks can do it themselves. It can't be so hard. I can practise right now. By the time you open tonight, I'll be real slick. Gimme a whole tray of fish and I'll de-bone em right now. Na, na, na, he says, you gotta do it *at the table*. It's not *what* you do, it's how you do it. I need someone with showmanship, he says. So why not hire a showman? I say. He shows me out. At the noodle house they say, Sorry, gotta have black hair. Maybe you dye your hair, make up your eyes, come back next week. Next week I won't get into their uniforms. At the pizza joints, all ten of them, they shrug, point at their empty tables, tell me to come back in the fall. At the Jewish place they want me to sing, in Yiddish for Chrissakes, in between shifts. And I don't need to tell ya about the clubs – only body-builders in leotards get an interview.

Can I mix drinks, mister? Sure. Fix a wicked Bloody Mary, a lethal Godfather. How come nobody wants a waitress just to serve food around here?

Could have asked pa for a loan, but I wouldn't have got it, not without spilling the beans. I can lie, but not to pa, and the truth – he couldn't take it, not since ma ran off. Never forgave her for deserting him. Never forgave me my lack of ambition. Drop-outs disgust him. Deserters disgust him. He drives me crazy. He'd think I'd flipped. Coming all this way to get rid of it. Find me a shrink if he found out. Talks about the weight of responsibility like it was some kind of blessing. Some blessing.

I'm ambitious now. My own life in my own small – but not squalid – apartment. That's what I'm aiming at. Me plus a kid equals welfare, standing in line for handouts. And charity from pa. And that equals defeat. So many calculations. Had plenty time for calculations. Three hundred bucks – it ain't a lot around here. Coupla nights maybe, in the right place. This place has gotta be it. So cool and dark. A week. A week at the outside. Gotta be. A chance, I need a fast chance. And a drink of water.

Hell, Alma swung it for me. Not that she'd have encouraged me if she'd known. If she'd known I'd have got her schpiel about the sanctity of life and the rights of the unborn while we folded napkins. But maybe she guessed. Seven months gone herself and still shifting trays. Told her I was taking a vacation. She was happy. Needs all the overtime and tips available. Hasn't had a vacation in eight years, not since she hitched up with Prescott, the chronic student. Eight years of college fees to find and she a waitress on minimum wage. It'd make you cry. And in a nickel and dime joint like Marty's, Jesus. Prescott finally got wise when Alma showed him one of his own fertility graphs. Her chances of becoming a mother had gotten as slim as his own of ever finishing his research. She reckoned they'd better strike before the iron froze. Alma's smart – knows everything Prescott knows, and some. But Alma don't know what she wants.

I know no one wants me to keep it, not really. No one knows, not even Harry. He ain't been by in two months anyhow and, Jeez, if he got wind of it he'd cross the state line as fast as you could say gestation. Maybe that bitch at the clinic would like me to see it through. That way I'd make her job easier. One less termination to arrange. One less phone call.

I could sleep right now, it's so cool and dark. A week's work. Fire me after a week but it's gotta be now, can't come back next week. Next week's too late, heatwave or no heatwave. Can't think about it any longer. Each day it's harder to believe it can be got rid of, terminated. As if it's just a matter of flicking a switch, on, off, gone. Gotta be done before I start guessing at its gender. Before it's too late. Before I begin to picture a face. Before I can't face it.

You're my last stop, mister, I can't do this one more time. I'm getting lockjaw from this goddamn smile. And my feet. Jesus. Not one more time today. Maybe tomorrow I'll go all the way up 3rd and all the way down 4th. Maybe. But today this is the end of the line. Not another threshold, not another lobby, even a cool one like this. Not another, Hi, I'd like to speak with the manager.

Positive, gotta act positive. Today's word. Today negative sounds a whole lot better. Gonna do it this time. Gonna say, Hi, I'm Joanne Lemme, Miss Joanne Lemme, experienced waitress, knowledge of steaks, seafood, Italian, Puerto Rican, Greek, Chinese, formal service, casual service, bar service, brisk service, service always with a smile. You name it, mister, I'll do it. I can sing, dance, rollerskate. My work record's clean as a fresh tablecloth. Anything you want. Gota spare dress with me, but I'm average size, fit any uniform. Worked all over town. Sure thing. Just dropped in to check you out. Felt like a change, you know. Liked the look of your place. Real nice place you got here. I tell ya, I chose it. Said to myself, this looks like a fine place to work. There's no problem, mister, no problem. Thought you might be hiring, that's all. Thought you might have a start for a waitress. Lemme start tonight, mister, I'm all set. All I need's a glass of water. It's hot out there.

Any kids? he'll say.

No, sir, no kids whatsoever.

DRIFTER

FIONA HAD KEPT MOVING WEST IN the hope that home ties would stretch and thin out like rubber bands until they snapped, leaving her free to hang loose in the new country, on the temperate shores of the Pacific. At times homesickness stopped her in her tracks – flashes of dark tenements blotting out a sunny Canadian day, monochrome shots of Glasgow, Scotland, in her mind's eye a hungry beast of a city, crouched over the wide dirty Clyde. Voices, accents from home, unchanged after decades, heard at bus terminals, in the stacked aisles of supermarkets, they could be ignored. The Scots were all over Canada. It was at other times, when she was least expecting it, least prepared, that homesickness washed over her like a wave and then she wanted nothing except to be swept on through eight hours of Greenwich Mean Time, back to the city from which she had escaped.

That was what she'd called it, escape, and it had been exciting, running off to a new country with her young man, with talk of marriage, great job prospects, a house of their own.

The longer she had been gone, the darker home became

in her mind. The city at night – its tight knot of empty office blocks, its locked parks, desolate gap-sites where old homes had been torn down and new homes had not yet been built – its only brightness the dazzling motorway which shot through the dark heart of it all.

The door of the Amanda is open to the street. The rain is slanting across the doorway like rods of neon. Inside, the bar is dingy, noisy, ugly. The R & B band play flat and raw, beardless boys grinning through songs of death, destruction and state penitentiaries. On the dance-floor, Joe, ex-jockey from Alabama, is showing Nelly how much better than the youngsters he can jive, his wiry body squirming like a weasel's, his eyes bright with cunning. Nelly looks like she's loving it all.

At the table nearest the dance-floor, next to Fiona, sits Tamara. She is shaking her rat-tail hair in time to the band. Tamara is very young, serious, scruffy.

'I was brought up in an atmosphere of violence, sexual violence, I mean my dad never raised a hand to my mom but it was there, I know it was there. My boyfriend needs to really get inside my sociology for things to work out between us. My singing helps me keep it all together and hang loose. I sing blues but no sexist shit, you know. I write my own lyrics about the environment, the trees and the water and the Indians and the whales. And sexual violence, you know there's a lot I have to sing about. I want people to hear these things so maybe I can do some good. Maybe someone out there hears what I'm saying. I do these voice exercises so I can sing real low, like a black woman. That's what I really wanna do, to sing like a black woman. But I don't dig some

black women's blues, I mean the old stuff, Bessie Smith, Billie Holiday, I guess those women were real messed up too. I mean you listen to the lyrics and some of the lyrics are real sexist. I guess they must have sold out to make money. I don't care about money at all. I'll never sell out, not my music. I'm recording my songs when I feel it's the right time, like timing's real important. The moon influences everything we do, I mean look at the tides, look at that huge ocean, the moon influences that huge ocean, so think what it can do to us little people. That's why I like living out west where I can be part of that huge thing, that moontide. The Pacific waves are deep, they influence my music on a real deep level. I'm calling my songs Wise Womanist Blues.'

Beneath the bridges of Glasgow, bridges named after trading posts of the old days – Jamaica Bridge, Kingston Bridge, names which as a child spoke to her of sugar and spice, though nowadays reggae music and ganja are more profitable exports – beneath the bridges, the river at night flowed black and viscous as crude oil, with its greasy yellow sheen, the river which had swallowed bodies and hoarded the ghosts of shipyard workers, meths drinkers, wild careless children, desperate mothers, reckless teenagers, bankrupt businessmen, existential students, failed painters, defeated boxers, distracted lovers, pleasure sailors, US Navy personnel, gamblers, debtors, people whose secrets had been found out, people whose secrets were about to be found out, quiet, lonely people who had no secrets and couldn't foresee ever having any. Those who fell and those who were pushed.

Fiona is at the table with friends, new friends, women she has dragged out of their domestic worlds for a night on the town, women who only see each other when Fiona calls round in her beat-up car which she can barely afford to run but runs anyway, so she can do things like this, so she can offer her friends a ride, and so she can clatter up the highway twice a month to meet Kent in his mother's cluttered apartment with its lamps which blow fuses every time they use the place and clocks which chime every fifteen minutes, warning that time is moving on willy-nilly and if she doesn't get her act together here, now, between one chime and the next, the past will catch up with the present and the future will be written up as appointments in Kent's diary (under Gym).

She had arranged things with Kent from the beginning. They met while his wife Diane was on a trip to Europe. Kent omitted to mention the existence of Diane until he and Fiona had gone well past being strangers in the night. Not that they had gone much further than meeting for sex – on his mother's bed – his wife's photo in his wallet, and his daughter's.

He brought his toilet bag. She brought food, wine and flowers for the waxed dining table. And bedsheets. In Kent's mother's apartment were trunks full of linen – embroidered pillowcases, bolster rolls, eiderdowns, patch-work quilts – but even though she was unlikely to return from the nursing home, Fiona brought her own bedsheets, which Kent thought bizarre but Fiona knew was sim-ply superstitious. A sinner should not leave traces and screwing a married man, worse, being in love with him, was, in her mind – put there long ago and never rooted out – sinful. And sin, though she would never use the *word* in any seriousness, brought with it guilt. And guilt, like the ragged insistent chimes of too many clocks, came round again and again.

But you have to have fun once in a while and tonight everyone is really trying hard to do just that. Nobody minds that the band is mediocre or that the place is drab. Nobody seems to notice. It's a change, it's new to them, that's the thing, that's what west-coast living is about, being somewhere new, somewhere young. Everyone at the table is from somewhere else, though none is as far from home as Fiona.

The big break across the Atlantic had its difficult moments, but the rest was easy, easy once she ceased being Fiona Fell of Maryhill, Glasgow, Scotland, and became just another landed immigrant, a drifter. Apart from other expatriate Scots, people she met often didn't know where her country was, far less her city. And after she'd described the weather and the lack of work, most people didn't enquire further, so it was easy to let the old loyalties and irritations peel off, old skin left in the old country. After the initial wrench, loosening her mother's hands from her neck, rubbing the ache where her mother's fingers had clung on until she had to break away, to escape by bus, train, plane from all that was so familiar it was invisible until those final moments. Invisible and then suddenly and painfully vivid. She'd said she'd write often and come home for visits. She'd said she'd be able to save the fare in no time if wages were as good as Donnie had been told.

After the farewell, turning away from her mother's tearful smiles and her father's unsteady handshake, the rest was casual, accidental, easy. There was everything to look forward to and she was impatient to be away, to be with Donnie, who would be waiting in the departure lounge.

'Don't be late,' he had joked, 'or I'll go without you.' But in the end it was she who had gone on without Donnie.

They were both in the new world still, but now three thousand miles and a $500 round-trip ticket apart. When the marriage fell apart – so much water under the bridge now was all she'd say of it – she had pushed on west, a year here, six months there, taking in all seven years to cross Canada. Donnie settled into east-coast city ways which kept him working long hours to make the rent, blowing out on stimulants every weekend to compensate and never getting around to seeing all those places he'd told Fiona about.

Fiona had seen plenty places, met plenty people. She had addresses all over Canada – a bed or at least a floor for the night if she were to go back east on a visit. It was all there and she had taken part, had joined in wherever she found herself, working at whatever was to hand, joining associations: unions and women's groups, the peace movement. She had reached her destination, the west. There was no doubt it was beautiful and also, as far as accommodation was concerned, this time she had been lucky. Not another crummy apartment but a house, with gleaming hardwood floors and a view: sailboats moored in the bay, ferries ploughing across the Strait, tree-covered islands close up and in the distance, glittering snow-capped peaks. But part of her couldn't quite acclimatise to the abundance of everything, the forests so tall and strong, the berry bushes so laden with fruit, the supermarket shelves piled high with bulk-buy value packs. Part of her remained inert. A hard dark seam ran through her.

Joe is dancing with Sharon who intently ignores his encouraging winks and jabbing, bony elbows. Nelly has returned to the table, flushed from dancing. She smoothes down her hair with her hands, making it neat – like the rest of her – neat, clean, with the kind of scrubbed look which comes from hours spent outdoors, tending vegetables and fixing up her cheap but decrepit house.

'I put one bucket under the real big hole and emptied it each morning until I could borrow my neighbour's ladder to go up and do something temporary about the shingles and then another drip got going in Casey's bedroom so I moved his bed and put the paint tray down to catch the splashes. Then last night when the rain begins again I see two new puckers in the ceiling and I think, Oh my God, the whole house is gonna fall in on me and Casey, we're gonna be drowned in our beds and Ronnie's not due home for a month and there's no money to pay for a new roof anyway until next spring – and I'm wondering how much longer is this rain gonna go on falling, it just seems like it's never gonna stop, it's a flood, a slow, dreary flood, seeping in from all sides, tunnelling through the cracks like a plague of worms, rotting the roots of my carrots and beets, eating away my home. But I love the summer here, I really love the summer and I guess we need some of this rain. At least we don't have the cold they get back east. Deep down I'm a pioneer at heart and a pioneer's gotta put up with some tough times. My grandparents had it real tough when they came to Canada from Holland. Dirt poor, they were. Dropped off on the Prairies with a logpile and told to get building a house for themselves before winter came

and snowed them under. They had everything to learn. My grandfather was a postman back home and my grandmother was a seamstress – what did they know about housebuilding? But between them they knocked up a shack for themselves and it gave them shelter from the snow which that winter banked up around them to the rafters. Deep down I just love it here on the island. Even the rain can be kind of neat, I mean. I get the stove going and pull in the sofa and sit all evening drinking tea and reading long novels. Trilogies are my favourite. It's so neat to meet up with a character in a new setting, it's just like coming out tonight and meeting everybody again. Oh my God, it's so good to get out. And I just love this band.'

Nelly, Tamara, Sharon, Fiona. Apart from Fiona, they lived with men, for better or worse. Fiona knew that none of them was ecstatic about her life, having spent many an hour in her apartment – a popular refuge for Nelly, Tamara and Sharon – listening late into the night to the troubles of her friends, offering advice and tea. It was good to feel useful, good to feel part of others' lives but it wasn't enough. And the situation with Kent was hopeless. She was cut off from any normal access, obliged to be a woman in waiting. It wasn't enough any more. There had been times when it might have been, when life was light and men were disposable but now when she looked forward, the future looked lonely. No children, no work – she hadn't counted on unemployment here – and no man. It wasn't enough.

Sharon returns to the table by herself. Joe meanders back towards the table but instead of sitting down, continues on to the bar, patting Fiona's back as he passes, letting her know with a nudge and a shoulder squeeze that he hasn't forgotten her, the first woman at the table to speak to him, the one responsible for his array of dancing partners.

'That guy!' says Sharon. 'It's hard to believe he and Brad are the same species. Know what he said to me? "I must be the luckiest guy in the room to have all you ladies at my table." I mean, he joined us. And nobody invited him. "All you ladies." Does he think he's going to take us all home with him? But I mean, I just can't imagine Brad ever in his life coming out with such dumb lines. Or Nelly's Ronnie. Or even Tamara's Crazy Dave. Or Kent. Been seeing him at all? It must be tough him being so unavailable but really, a man can be too available. It's important to be on your own. If I don't find time in the day for myself, just to sit down in my home, alone, I get stressed, know what I mean? I start to feel this ache up around the back of my neck and my head goes kind of stiff and my jaw starts to hurt and I feel like my lips are drawn tight across my face, exposing my teeth, that I'm like a trapped animal, all tied up inside, ready to spring. That's when Brad and the kids know they'd better get the hell out of the house. But usually it doesn't come to that because deep down we get along pretty well. We're family. It must be a whole lot different for you. I heard – but maybe you know already – that Kent and Diane aren't getting along. They're sleeping apart, which says something. Do you reckon he'll leave her? But maybe you wouldn't want that, you've got your own life, keep yourself busy, know so many people, do so many things. I wish I had the time for activities, but with the job and Brad and the kids, the days seem to fill up so fast. You can do so much more if you're independent. When

42

Brad and I are fighting I really think I'd like to be alone again. But then I meet a guy like Joe and I'm thankful I'm not.'

Now it is Fiona's turn to push through the cluster of wet-eyed drunks, swaying and sweating at the edge of the dance-floor, heads jerking like puppets in time to the music. Joe is close up behind her, pushing her through the crowd with his skinny fingers, rubbing up against her with his narrow thighs, his jeans dragging against her skirt with a crackle of static.

They reach the dance-floor. Fiona turns to him and begins to speak. He can't hear what she's saying because of the music so she cups her hand over his ear and repeats,

'I think I'll pass on this dance.' Joe mimes his disappointment. It is comical, exaggerated, false but still he takes her arm and attempts to lead her on to the floor.

'Tamara likes to dance,' says Fiona but he still can't hear her, so she breaks away, arcs her palm across her face in a brisk, farewell wave and weaves through the dancers to the street door. Outside, she turns down one side street and another, glancing back to make sure that Joe hasn't followed her, cuts back to where her car is parked, climbs in and drives off along the streets, wet and black as rivers, towards the beckoning fountain of light at the highway intersection, with no direction in mind which feels like home.

CHILD'S PLAY

I'M LEARNING MY LESSON. I'M NOT even supposed to be playing with you, Arabella, so sit up like a good girl or I'll have to put you to bed and you'll be in disgrace. That's what I'm in. I know it's dark. I'm not allowed the light on because that's not disgrace. Being in the dark's disgrace. Doing nothing's disgrace. If anybody comes I'll have to hide you under the covers.

You'd cry if you were a crying doll but you don't have the bit inside for crying. Sonya, that's Wendy's doll, cries real tears if you put water in her mouth. She's got a key in her back for the noise. Sonya wets her pants as well. It's the same water. She cries and wets at the same time. That's what Jenny did today, before the lump stuck and the van came and she went away with the fairies. People have a lump in the throat for crying. It grows until the water comes out of your eyes unless you can hold it in. Holding it in is brave but Jenny held it in too long. You've got to swallow it.

I wanted a doll like Sonya but she was too dear so I got you. Wendy's richer. I'm not poor but I'm not rich, I'm comfortable. That's because of sacrifices. My mum says

44

poor people don't know about sacrifices. Jenny Pilly's poor. She's here today and gone tomorrow. Jenny's mum's a fly-by-night. She does the moonlight flit. She doesn't like the scheme so she goes gallivanting. The scheme's at the end of our street but our street's not the scheme. That starts after the witch's house. The witch flies by night too but she doesn't really fly, she sits on her broom. Running up the witch's path and ringing her doorbell is brave. If she catches you, you turn into a dead bird on her fireplace.

I'm not allowed on the scheme. The houses only have numbers, not names as well. Our house is detached. That means it's got a gate and a hedge with a garden right round the house and it's got two doors and it's alone. If a house has a Siamese twin it's a semi. My mum doesn't like semis and houses with numbers.

I don't want to rub shoulders with Tom, Dick and Harry.

My mum says that. I've never seen people rubbing shoulders. Cows do it when they're itchy but people can scratch themselves.

Are you listening, Arabella? I'm going to be strict with you for your own good. You'll thank me when you're older. I'm learning my lesson so you've got to learn yours. I've got the slipper right here, my girl. I'm keeping my eye on you. I don't like it, Arabella, it hurts me more than you. Now give Mummy a kiss, or I'll give you away to the tinks.

Wendy's been my best friend for a whole week. Wendy hates Jenny Pilly so I've got to hate her too.

> Jenny Pilly's not just silly
> She's a guttersnipe
> She's got nits and chappy lips
> And all she gets to eat is tripe.

Wendy sang her song in the playground, loud, and Jenny's face turned red and she said a swear. Wendy sang it again, louder, and this time Jenny grabbed Wendy's jotter and wrote SNOBBY TITS on it with a red pencil. The teacher's the only one who's allowed to use a red pencil, except in art. Wendy was nearly crying, she had the lump in her throat but not the water in her eyes. Dunkie Begg got the strap for scribbling BUMS on his jotter. TITS is the same as BUMS, it's dirty. So is PISS. And FANNY is worse than dirty, it's disgusting. So don't ever let me hear you saying that word Arabella, if you do learn to talk, or there will be trouble.

Look at you. What a tyke you are. You're as bad as Jenny. I'll have to send you away to live on the scheme if this goes on, or else I'll give you away to the tinks, wait and see. A tink will turn you into brass or she'll take you everywhere in the rag-bag or she'll give you to her baby with the runny nose. She doesn't even have a house on the scheme, you know. She's not got a penny to her name, just bits of gold in her teeth.

Tinks are tykes and guttersnipes are common hussies. Hussies are a sort of lady, like starlings are a sort of bird. Hussies paint their toe-nails and paint the town red. When Jenny's mum paints the town red, Jenny gets to stay up really late. My mum has a special voice for hussies, a faraway voice. The lady in the chemist's, the one with the white lipstick, she's a hussy. When my mum buys toothpaste and the lady wraps it up, my mum says thank you to the shelf.

Don't roll your eyes like that, Arabella. If the wind changes they'll stick that way – you'll be cross-eyed and see everything back to front. Jenny could only see stars until the man brought the gas mask. That wasn't supposed to be the consequences. But now she can stay off school. Jenny's not good at anything at school. She's nearly always bottom. If I'm not top or nearly top I'm in disgrace but when Jenny was bottom her mum gave her sweets. Sweets are better than a rose from the inkblock. You get the rose for five gold stars but you can't do anything with it.

I told my mum about the sweets for being bottom and she said that's the sort of thing riff-raff do. And my dad said birds of a feather flock together. That's a saying. It means people are like birds, there's different kinds, like doves and starlings. With people it's riff-raff which are never-never and common which are undesirable and god-fearing which are respectable and comfortable. Poor ones have faces like marbles and rich ones are rough diamonds. You'll be clever like me if you learn all the words.

Jenny lives in a flat on the never-never. Her name's in a book. We got a story once about never-never land where nobody ever grew up but it wasn't about the scheme. There's lots of old people on the scheme and you've got to grow up to be old. Jenny's never-never is having your name ticked off in a book. A man comes to your house with the book and a suitcase. Sometimes he has a dog with him that's nearly a wolf. You've got to give him money.

47

The Clean-Ezy man comes to our house and the Onion Johnny but not the man with the suitcase. He doesn't go to Wendy's house either, the tick man.

My mum likes me to play with Wendy. She's the lesser of two evils. Her dad's a rough diamond. So is Mr de Rollo next door. He's got lots of shiny things in his house and a silver car which sparkles in the dark, like the stars. He's a dark horse. He made himself by climbing out of the gutter. He's got liquid gold in a bottle. It's a drink. My dad loves Mr de Rollo's liquid gold. But the man's got no breeding, he says. Mrs de Rollo's really young. She's got blonde hair out of a bottle.

> Breeding is what birds do once they've got a nest.
> Breeding is how you tell the sheep from the goats.

I told you Arabella, you'll be cross-eyed. You'll see everything all wonky, like when you look at the magic mirrors at the shows. One blows you up fat like a balloon and one makes you long and thin like a clothes-pole and one makes you turn wavy. It's not like the witch's magic. If they had a mirror that turned you rich if you were poor, that would be real magic. But if you were rich to begin with, you'd have to turn poor. Jenny would turn into Wendy and Wendy would turn into Jenny. I'd have to turn into somebody but I couldn't turn rich or poor from comfortable. I'd be like the wavy mirror. Jenny could be my best friend instead of Wendy.

If Jenny was my best friend, maybe I wouldn't have to write Thank-You letters. She never has to. I have to write if I get a present, always, even if it's horrible, and say it's lovely. My mum says I mustn't look a gift horse in the mouth. Auntie Eunice is a gift horse but I never see her so I can't look her in the mouth. Probably she's got huge teeth like real horses. Anyway she always sends me fawn tights and I hate fawn. One time I asked my mum if I could get a present on the never-never, so I could send it back if I didn't like it. She said the day that happens will be over her dead body, which means no way. She says that about me staying up to watch the grown-up programmes. Jenny's allowed to but I'm not because they're tripe and tripe is common. There's lots of kissing and crying but the kissing is unsuitable. On the television people kiss on the lips. They go on for ages and it's truelove.

Truelove is unsuitable.

The kissing I do isn't truelove because I don't get kissed back. It's a Thank-You kiss or an I'm-Sorry kiss and it's really only half a kiss. Somebody turns their face to the side and I've got to do it to their cheek. Cheek-by-jowl. It's the same when I'm in disgrace, my mum won't kiss back.

They don't have disgrace at Sunday School, just at real school and at home. You don't have to be quiet or good at tests and have breeding. You just have to give away all your clothes to the tinks and the loving shepherd will save you, even if you're bad. That's because of magic. They've got that mirror, see. It's very far away. It's in the kingdom of heaven where you never die. But you've got to be dead to get there maybe. You can even give away fawn tights from Auntie Eunice and it's not ungrateful because it's better to give than to receive. See, the poor inherit the earth. That means they get the world when the rich people die. The rich people turn poor and go to the kingdom of heaven and the poor inherit the world. The world becomes heaven on earth. That's the magic and nobody has to live on the scheme anymore.

It's because of magic I'm in disgrace. See, there's different kinds of magic. There's flying on a broom and magic mirrors and there's the kind Wendy does to people if they don't do the dare. It's called You Are Getting Sleepy and I was holding Jenny's arms behind her back so Wendy could do the magic with her fingers. Wendy must have done too much of the trick because you're not supposed to hit your head and see stars. You're just supposed to fall asleep and wake up as Wendy's slave. Jenny didn't wake up at all. Not even when the Jani did the kiss of life, not even when they put the gas mask on her face. Jenny's in the dark now, like me, but she's not in disgrace. She can't see even with her eyes open.

I've got to learn my lesson.

> The kingdom of heaven is over my dead body.
> Rough diamonds thank their lucky stars.
> Guttersnipes are undesirable.
> Birds of a feather are elements.
> Fly-by-nights are dark horses.
> Spare the rod and spoil the consequences.
> Breeding makes you comfortable.
> Riff-raff rub shoulders.
> Never-never land is gone to the dogs.

Have you got that, Arabella?

BEFORE OSCAR

'I SUPPOSE YOU'RE TIRED.'
  'What do you think?'
  'And want some sleep.'
  'That's all I'm fit for.'
  'So what's new?'

They couldn't really afford it but something had to be done and if blowing some cash on a weekend away might brighten up their marriage, Rod and Belinda were prepared to give it a go.

The hotel is better than they had expected: a true stone's throw from the beach with unobstructed sea views from every window; calm, comfortable furnishings; a varied and appetising menu; childwatch facilities allowing parents to linger over dinner in the evenings and – as the hotel brochure puts it – rediscover romance. The sun shines. The air is fresh. The omens are good.

Oscar has already made the long, carpeted corridors and the wide staircase his playground. He clambers up and down and up and down the stairs, squealing with glee each time he reaches the top step and jumping off the third step up when he reaches the bottom. Rod sips a pre-lunch gin and tonic, occasionally glancing over at his blond, two-year-old son who looks so like him, savouring the warm flush of alcohol and fatherly pride.

Upstairs, Belinda unpacks. She holds up her swimsuit – a sky-blue one-piece. Would she fit it now? Stylish when new, now three years old and still unworn, bought shortly before Oscar began to stretch her belly and inflate her thighs. Before Oscar, Belinda would have been the first on the beach to peel off her clothes and parade by the water's edge, working out with gusto, displaying her muscle tone and as much else as local beach restrictions would allow. Before Oscar, fitness was Belinda's religion. She attended aerobics classes, yoga classes, cycled to work, ate sensibly, drank only the occasional glass of dry white wine. Her goals in life centred on slowing her resting pulse rate to a virtual standstill and ridding herself of anything – hair, flesh, garments – superfluous. Before the act of conception she was a health visitor's dream and the envied ideal of many.

Now, slim trim Belinda inhabits an idle body, a slack skin. She lounges at every available opportunity, smokes heavily and matches her husband's consumption of gin, wine, brandy.

She puts her swimsuit back in the wardrobe. It isn't fully summer yet so she won't have to expose her body to the beach if she doesn't want to. And Rod, she knows, won't strain himself attempting to persuade her.

Lunch is a selection of cold meats and salad, with optional french fries, which Rod orders for himself and Oscar. Oscar claps his hands and shouts *chips, chips, chips*, until his food arrives. Belinda watches, as if to strengthen her resolve, as Rod squirts ketchup over his stack of carbohydrates. She picks at her starch-free meal, then gives up tormenting herself and looks out to sea but this doesn't help. The frothy waves remind her of meringue, the clouds of ice-cream.

'My wife will have the fruit salad,' Rod tells the waitress, a fresh-faced girl who lispingly addresses him as 'Sir' and then giggles. Rod and Oscar have crème-caramel for dessert and Belinda sneaks a spoonful from Oscar while her husband orders more drinks from the waitress.

'Good service,' Rod remarks as he watches the girl trot off to the bar, her trim young hips swinging. Belinda's bite of pudding sticks in her throat. Had Rod always looked at other women, not to mention girls, before she lost her ideal figure, before Oscar? Oscar tugs at her sleeve again and again before she turns to him.

'Good pudding,' he says, and lovingly offers his Mummy another bite.

Though it is early in the season, the beach is fairly busy with the usual games and activities. Belinda unrolls a beach mat, spreads it out in a sheltered dune, lies down and opens a thick paperback. Rod and Oscar begin to kick a ball between them. Rod enjoyed this part of being a father, enjoyed having the boy to fool around with, when he could take time out for it. He just couldn't take much time out.

Rod's work kept him long hours at the office. He left home early in the morning and returned late, usually after Oscar's bedtime. Each evening, before Belinda put him to bed, Oscar would hover at the door, tearfully asking when Daddy would be home. When he didn't get the answer he wanted, he laid into one of his toys. When Rod returned, Oscar would have given up struggling against sleep, Belinda would have quickly tidied away the toys and prepared a meal. She and Rod would eat, drink a little too much and resume their non-conversation carried over from the previous night. Rod was away too much, Belinda at home too much. Nothing was ever resolved. Night followed night with stunning monotony. Sex had become rapid, perfunctory, joyless.

Belinda begins to doze face down on the mat. The noises of the beach swim together in her ears: the gulls, a radio, voices, bare feet thudding softly in the sand. Smells fill her nostrils: of seaweed, suntan oil, hamburgers frying on a pavement stand. Everything is as expected. The breeze dusts her arms with fine white sand. Its coolness tickles her skin. Belinda leaves her surroundings behind and enters a hazy world where the edges have melted, where she is both herself and the elements, where she is rock, sand, sea, heat, sunlight, where she blends in totally.

Oscar breaks the spell when he leaps on to her back.

'Gee up, Mummy. Gee up.'

'Where's Daddy?'

'Daddy gone. Daddy gone.' Oscar's ball blows along a trail of footprints in the sand.

'Where did Daddy go? Did Daddy tell Oscar where he was going?' Oscar's blue eyes turn to the horizon. His mouth opens as if to speak but no information follows.

'Which way did Daddy go?'

'Daddy's a man, Mummy's a lady,' is Oscar's reply.

Belinda scans the beach. Couldn't Rod have told her where he was going? They might have all gone exploring, together, as a family. That was the point of the weekend, after all, to spend time together.

'Mummy's a lady. A angry lady.'

'Daddy's a naughty boy,' Belinda replies. Oscar grins.

'Oscar's a naughty boy, too?'

'No. Oscar's a good boy. Let's make a sandcastle.'

'Sandcastle! Sandcastle! Sandcastle!' Oscar bounces up and down in anticipation as Belinda picks a clean stretch of sand and tries a sample castle. The sand slides out of the bucket as perfectly as a sponge pudding. Belinda imagines it spooned open and oozing syrup. Her stomach feels cheated by her low-calorie lunch.

'You feel lousy because you're out of shape.' Rod's phrase repeats on her but she continues to feel hungry. For food, sex, affection.

'Mummy?'

'Here's the bucket. You try now.' Belinda looks on as her son, his tongue sticking out in concentration, begins to dig.

When Oscar is looking for a flag for his castle, he finds, in the assorted rubbish at the tide line, a used sheath.

'Pink balloon, Mummy.' He drags her over to see and his mouth droops in disappointment when she won't blow it up for him. Belinda kicks Oscar's find into a pile of driftwood. Had the sea thrown it up from some far-flung beach or was it the flotsam from a midnight mating on that very spot? Before Oscar, before their marriage, she and Rod might have been the lovers on the beach, chancing discovery, excited by that chance. Their meetings had begun as that kind of affair, with appointments and secrecy, with spontaneous acts of lust, with Rod's first wife in the background. Guilt and thrills. Sex and more sex. Gifts representing love.

Rod has been gone for most of the afternoon. The sun is casting longer shadows and the breeze is blowing up again. Oscar has his coat and shoes on but still fills his bucket and tips lopsided turrets around the wall which Belinda built for him. Belinda is down on her hands and knees, scooping up the sand. She has built a large oval mound, about the size of a dinghy. With fingernails and a sharp stone she begins to scrape and chip at it. A smaller oval appears at the top. Soon it has cork eyes, a pebble nose, scallop-shell lips and seaweed hair, wild and curly like her own.

'Face!' says Oscar. 'Hair,' then returns to his fort. Belinda works on, unaware of the time. She gouges a deep cleavage between two full breasts, embedding in each a limpet for a nipple. The more she works on her woman of sand, the larger she grows. She packs the belly, slapping it into shape until it is smooth and swollen and solid. She presses on a bottle-neck navel.

'More seaweed, Mummy,' says Oscar, handing her a soggy strand. 'There, Mummy,' he says and lays it between the carved fingers.

'Right,' she says. 'Only you can't see it when the hands are there.'

'Is it hiding?'

'Yes, it's hiding.'

'Peekboo!' Oscar runs round in circles.

A cool blast of wind blows the loose sand in their faces. Oscar shivers. Belinda fastens his jacket, pulling the hood over his ears. His lips are tinged with blue. She hadn't noticed the drop in temperature. She has let her child become chilled. She feels guilty.

As soon as they return to the hotel, she bundles him into a warm bath and rubs him down with a flannel. The boy shivers for a little but soon becomes absorbed in building bath-water castles.

It takes Belinda nearly an hour to settle the child into sleep. The strange room, strange cot, the distant rumble of waves on the beach, the clatter and laughter drifting up from the bar, distract him. His eyes stare into the darkness as he listens and listens, until his eyelids eventually droop and his limbs relax. Belinda turns up the intercom on the child alarm and creeps out of the room.

She is wearing a jungle-print dress and several heavy bangles which clank together when she moves. For a brief moment, crossing the dining-room to where Rod is waiting for her, Belinda enjoys the sensation of heads turning as she passes. A big bold woman in a big bold dress.

What could happen next is that, relaxing over a leisurely meal – as the hotel brochure has it – Rod and Belinda might attempt to iron out the creases in their marriage and perhaps restore some of the intimacy which has been absent since they became parents. And ceased being lovers. Their relationship has been rerouted via Oscar. Their conversations, routines, outings, revolve around Oscar. Their bed is often shared with him. Belinda and Rod have made room in their lives for the child but in doing so, have moved apart from each other.

'Did you forget your black suit?' says Rod. Belinda sits down, deflated.

'What's wrong with this dress?'

'It's fine.'

'You mean you don't like it?'

'I said it's fine. If you want to be conspicuous.'

Rod doesn't want Belinda to be conspicuous. At least not in her present, far from perfect condition. His eyes stray from her array of checks and dots and zigzags to the skimpy black tube into which the passing waitress has poured herself. It's the same girl who served them lunch, snaking her fat-free hips between the tables as she deposits baskets of breadsticks.

'Why didn't you say you wanted to go exploring?'

'You were sleeping.'

'How did you know?'

'Your eyes were closed. I thought you were sleeping.'

'I might have wanted to be wakened.'

'I didn't know that, did I?'

'You didn't think, did you?' Belinda plucks a breadstick and snaps it between her teeth.

Belinda settles the child down for a second time, having been summoned, half-way through her main course, by the childwatch service. When she arrived in the room Oscar was standing up in his cot, howling, his face red and glazed with tears. He sneezed. His nose ran. His forehead was hot. She felt guilty, again.

She tells him a story, made up from the events of the day.

'And then Oscar made a great big sandcastle . . .'

'Mummy made a great big lady,' adds Oscar.

'Just close your eyes and listen.'

'A great big Mummy. A great big huge gigantic Mummy lady.'

'It's late, Oscar . . .'

'Mummy's got a dress on!'

'Go to sleep now.'

'Pretty dress. Like it. Oscar like it.'

Belinda hugs him close to her on the single bed, enjoying his warmth, his sweet, child's breath on her face, his small fingers probing her ears, nose, mouth, curling into her hair, his sleepy voice continuing a story for which she had no ending. She is tempted to crawl under the covers and sleep. And as the boy's a little off-colour perhaps she should. But Rod, what about Rod? The father, the husband, the too-occasional lover, she couldn't leave him sitting on his own, could she? She, the mother, the wife, the would-be-if-she-were-asked lover. Was it possible to be all three? Was it even worth attempting?

As the child's breathing becomes slow and regular, Belinda tiptoes not to the door, but to the window. She slips between the curtains and looks out at the beach. It's dark and empty apart from a couple at the shoreline, in silhouette, arm in arm. At sea, a few spots of lights beam from distant boats.

As her eyes grow accustomed to the darkness, she begins to pick out a few more details on the beach. A deserted deck-chair, a fishcrate, a bleached sheep-skull, a dog – nose to the ground, tail erect, chasing a scent. Her eyes follow the dark frill of weed and junk at the tide line and there, a few yards inshore, is Oscar's fort and, nearby, brazenly exposing herself to the moon, the woman of sand.

Belinda's food is cold when she returns to the table. The sauce has congealed and the remains of the dish look unappealing but she eats it anyway, as Rod looks on. The diners are filtering through to the bar and the staff are setting empty tables for breakfast. Belinda's plate is whisked away as soon as she lays down her cutlery.

'What's for dessert?' she asks. The waitress glints at Rod and recites, 'Rum Babas with Fresh Cream and Egyptian Honey; Black Forest Gateau, with Swiss Cherries Marinated in Kirsch and Real Austrian Chocolate Icing; Avocado Cheesecake; Fresh Fruit Salad.'

Belinda eats her Rum Baba slowly, deliberately. Rod looks away, as if the sight of cream and rum-soaked batter disappearing into Belinda's mouth was mildly obscene.

'Before you say anything,' says Belinda, 'I don't want to hear it. I'm on holiday. I'm going to enjoy myself.'

'There are other ways.'

'Refresh my memory.'

'Well, you know, each to their own.'

'That's what I mean.'

Rod sighs – a superior, male sigh that says under its breath, Women! – and says, 'What exactly do you mean?'

'I *mean*, that's the way you like it. Each to their own. Self-satisfaction. Solo sex. It's lonely.'

'Are you drunk?' says Rod.

'Not yet,' says Belinda, as her husband rises from his chair and moves through to the bar, leaving Belinda to finish her dessert.

It is already late. The bar is noisy, busy. The band in the corner are still playing diluted versions of chart hits and two or three couples are clutching and shuffling round the floor. Rod is lingering at the bar, next to the dinner waitress who slithers on her stool and arches her young firm body in his direction.

Belinda wouldn't have thought of speaking to anyone but the view from her window seat is making her gloomy. Her thoughts are drifting out into the dark expanse of sea and conjuring up gales and shipwrecks. And it makes a change to be flattered, flirted with. Harmless enough. Only a lad after all and she's probably old enough to be his mother. And really it is her dress he likes, this lad with the even teeth and lean brown arms, who tells her his name is Tommy.

'Better than all that boring black,' he says. 'Who wants a tarty widow?'

'My husband,' says Belinda and that is the beginning of her revelations, made increasingly explicit through more drinks and Rod's extended absence.

'Don't think I don't love him. I do. And Oscar. Oscar more than anyone.'

The band switch from smooch to rock'n'roll. The groping couples huddle at the edge of the small dance-floor as Tommy and Belinda throw themselves about to a fast version of Johnny B Good. Belinda kicks off her shoes. Tommy loosens his shirt at the neck. Both of them are laughing. The stage lights wink in time.

Belinda wakes to Oscar pummelling her chest.

'Beach, Mummy. Want to go beach.'

Her head throbs from the previous night's drinks and the whispered row which continued long after the traffic announced morning. Her limbs are stiff from having squeezed in beside Oscar on the single bed to cut short the mutual recriminations. Rod snores on the double bed. Belinda considers smothering him with his pillow.

Oscar runs on ahead, catching sight of the flags on the castle he had made the day before. Belinda watches him running on, zigzagging, his arms wide like the wings of a bird or plane, pretending to be flying. For five minutes the previous night Belinda had felt that kind of freedom. Five minutes on the dance floor and the rest of the night trying to justify what Rod described as making an exhibition of herself. I needed it, she had tried to explain, but couldn't say exactly what she needed.

She can't believe it. She's down on her hands and knees in front of the sand woman, tears pricking her eyes. Her model has been desecrated. Someone has scratched FAT SLAG COW across the torso. The letters rip open the breasts and belly, like scars. The seaweed hair has been pulled from the head and piled at the groin. What had been a woman is now a bald monster, whose shell lips have been prised apart and stuffed with a shrivelled carrot, who has muck on her knees.

'Don't cry, Mummy.' When Belinda doesn't stop, Oscar too begins to cry.

'Castle OK,' he blubbers through his tears.

'So it is. The sandcastle's OK.'

Belinda stands up, her gaze still fixed on her poor defaced woman of sand. If it had been a boat, or a castle, if it had been anything else, maybe it wouldn't have cut her up like that, but it was a woman they'd done this to, a woman like her. There was no point in trying to repair the model. It was too far gone, wasn't it, and anyway, that kind of thing would only happen again.

'Fix the lady, Mummy. Fix the big Mummy lady. Please, Mummy.'

Belinda begins to scrape the dirt off the sand woman's knees. She dusts them with fresh sand. She takes a flat shell and begins to remodel the face. Oscar wipes away his tears of sympathy on the back of his sleeve. Before Oscar, Belinda would have given up on her woman of sand.

READING THE SHEETS

JAN IS AT THE WINDOW, DRESSED in the uniform of the hotel domestics – grey nylon overall and matching head-scarf, and her old flat black shoes that she keeps for work. Through the window she can see that it is just beginning to get light outside. A grey, misty glow spreads from the far coast over the still smooth water of the firth, wrinkled just a little as it approaches the near shore. It's a chilly morning. Jan stands over the clattering fan heater on the floor, letting the warm air blow around her knees. She yawns. She rubs some life back into her fingers, stiff from the drive over. Her car heater has broken. The car itself is a wreck, but it gets her to work, to the school, to the shopping centre, to meetings with her young man.

'Well, Missis. Daydreaming at this time of day?'
  'Morning, Annie.'
  'It's a cold one, right enough.'
  'So who's for off today?'
  'Most of them.'
  'We'll be on the sheets all morning then?'
  'No doubt.'

If it could all be sorted out as easily as the sheets – shoving the soiled pile into the tub, adding the detergent, the fabric softener, bleach, a touch of starch in the final rinse and they come out crisp and fresh for the next body to mess up. As good as new, nearly. Not that a single usually caused much disturbance. She'd gone in some mornings to strip down a single bed and could have sworn nobody had slept in it. And if she'd had a bad night with Chuck – and there'd been more than a few of them lately – and was feeling done in, it was so tempting just to plump up the pillows and straighten the quilt and say to hell with clean sheets but she hadn't given in to that kind of sloppiness yet. Clean sheets were one thing she'd insist on herself, if she stayed in a hotel. But singles were usually no trouble.

Doubles were a different story altogether. Like horoscopes and palms and that kind of thing, you could tell a lot about a couple by the state of the sheets. You could tell by the lie of them and where the sweat gathered what had been going on between the two, whether they'd made a night of it or just had a quick one before they went to sleep, whether they'd slept back to back or face to face, snuggled up close or on either edge of the bed. Of course stains were a giveaway and the things people left between the sheets had to be seen to be believed. Morna and Fay, the youngsters, got right into the whole business, reading the sheets they called it. They said they could tell how long a couple had been together, whether they were happy or not, and all kinds of other, cheekier details. They gave their sheet readings at tea-break and everybody got a good laugh about it, except old Annie who swore blind she shut her eyes when she stripped a bed, so she wouldn't see anything she shouldn't.

She wanted to give it all up and go back to the way things were before because they hadn't been so bad. Happily married? That was what everybody believed and even if it wasn't altogether true, if you said a thing often enough and had it echoed by everyone around you, you got to believing it yourself. And after so long it was hard to say whether it was you telling them or them telling you. Them being the family – her parents, Chuck's parents, the kids, their friends – who were mostly, apart from the girls at work, Chuck's friends and their wives. But after such a long time together you didn't expect to have much left that was just your own. And did anybody really want that? Didn't everybody want someone to share their little life with?

If Smiler had been pushy she'd have told him straight away where to get off. She had her knockback off pat after the time he'd helped her lug the laundry basket down the stairs and made some corny crack about getting in between the sheets with her. The next time he showed his face, lumbering about and getting in the way like a lad who'd grown too quickly and hadn't got used to his size, she'd tell him where to go. She'd tell him she was old enough to be his mother and she had enough trouble with her own kids as it was. But when he came back the next week, the bread tray balanced on his head, and knelt down on the floor so she could pick off the Halloween cake he'd brought for her kids – with a big grinning face on it, like his own – all she found to say was, I'm a happily married woman. And all he said was,

So I'm told, and went straight on to the kitchen with his
delivery.

*Jan pushes the trolley into the service lift, jams her foot in
the door until the heavy, cumbersome equipment fits in well
enough to close it. On the third floor she goes through the
reverse process, shoving the trolley out on to the carpet. A
few doors are open. Some of the guests are packed and dressed
to leave, others are still returning from breakfast. The leaving
routine is in process, adding to the usual cleaning work. Jan
enters the rooms after knocking, and asks the standard, Did you
enjoy your stay, Sir, Madam? She collects tips – to be pooled at
break, over tea and buns, cigarettes and gossip about the guests.
She goes through the rooms emptying waste-paper bins, picking
up the debris from the floors and the furniture, removing used
tumblers, soaps, face-flannels, towels, sheets.*

Chuck and Jan. Jan and Chuck. Fifteen years married,
happily by all accounts. Jan and Chuck, Elaine, Ailie and
Blair, six rabbits, a gerbil, a vegetable patch out the back.
The youngest of the three kids, Ailie, already eleven. The
time gone by without anyone noticing. And now, though
there were many happy anniversaries under the belt, it
was all going to have to fall apart.

Smiler and Jan. Jan and Smiler. They'd kept it quiet as
long as they could but nobody had any secrets in the hotel
for long and the girls were only too quick to notice that on
a Friday, delivery day, Jan had done her hair and put on a
bit of lipstick before coming to work. And who did that
to scrub around the laundry room at six in the morning?
Except Morna and Fay who were eighteen and man-daft.

And they – so Annie said – put their shock-pale panstick faces on at night and slept in them.

'Your toy boy's parking his wagon Jan.' Morna shouts it across the laundry and it's a signal for all the rest of them, Annie excepted, to whoop and cackle and for Jan's face to turn even redder than the steam makes it.

'Where's he taking you the day, Jan?'

'Must be somewhere flash. The boy's got his good jaikit on.'

'Tell us where you're off to. We'll come over and chamber.'

'Aye. And read your sheets.'

'Professional interest. We could test our theories on the pair of you. Then we'd know if we were on the right track.'

'You'd get a free trial offer.'

'We could start up a business.'

'Morna and Fay, sheet readers by appointment. Find your true partners through our unique and original method.'

'A photo of the two of you on our card. Smiler and Jan: two satisfied customers.'

'You lassies are over the score. What's between two people is nobody else's concern. When you get your own men, you'll find out why.'

'Ach, Annie. Fay's just jealous. She got stood up last night.'

'That doesn't surprise me.'

Jan loads up her trolley again with clean towels, washcloths, sheets, bars of soap and miniature bottles of shampoo and shower-gel. She is hurrying through her work as she always does on a

Friday so that she can add a few minutes on to the time they have together before Smiler has to drive back to work and she has to pick up Ailie from the school.

If only they could go somewhere half-decent, one of those cosy little places on the coast, decked out with nets on the ceiling and shiny brass lamps, maybe a bit of music playing softly in the background – nothing too mushy – where the waiter would bring over a menu and they could sit looking out at the water and laugh over the light unimportant things the other said, and when they'd ordered the food they'd become a bit more intimate and talk about all the things they'd like to do together. The food would arrive at their table, and after they'd eaten a bit and drunk some of the wine, they'd get a bit romantic. The afternoon would stretch out like the shadows on the water as they sat looking into each other's eyes every so often and smiling, hands touching above the table. They'd be feeling warm from the food and the wine and the closeness of their bodies. They wouldn't need to say much to each other by this time because being together was enough and anyway, they could tell what the other was thinking. And it wasn't boring, not the way knowing what someone else was thinking could be sometimes, for example with Chuck. Chuck never said anything interesting to her anymore.

'Here, Jan, the boy's away without saying hello. What's up with him the day?'

'Too good for us when he's all dressed up, eh?'

'D'you hear this Fay? Jan says the boy's behind with his deliveries.'

'Sounds serious, that. Has he been to the doctor about it, Jan?'

'A young man like that too, shame, eh? You and me'd better start looking at older men, Fay.'

Jan watches from the window as Smiler loads the empty trays into the back of the van, lowering them from his shoulders and sliding them into the racks, his tall body bent and awkward, tense, as he manoeuvres the trays of bread, pastries and fresh-cream gateaux. The bakery firm who employed him were famous in the area for fancy cream-cakes, so delicate items made up the bulk of his deliveries, which he loaded and unloaded, eased through badly-designed doors, up and down narrow staircases, through crowded corridors and hectic kitchens, and prevented from spoiling. Occasionally a couple of cakes collided on the tray, squashed together into a sticky mess. Smiler is more used to shifting large sturdy items – on previous driving jobs he'd carried bricks and cement.

If it had been the kind of fling Morna and Fay liked to think it was – Annie wouldn't even allow herself to imagine what went on – if it had been just a bit of fun, a bit on the side, that could have been taken care of easily enough. But that wasn't what it was all about really. That hardly came into it. The one and only time they'd actually gone to a hotel, it had been a wash-out, as far as that was concerned. If the girls had done their sheet reading after that night they'd have been, for once, dumbstruck.

The planning that had gone into that night. A whole night they'd managed to make for themselves. A small hotel far enough outside the area for them to be fairly sure of not being recognised. Smiler's wife off to her mother's with their boys, Chuck and the kids going camping up north. It had taken weeks to arrange, weeks of waiting, hoping that nothing would go wrong, that none of the kids would take ill, or the good weather break, or Smiler's wife cancel her trip. That had all worked out. They met at the crossroads, where she left her car, drove to the place, excited, impatient to be there, alone together, nervous as two virgins.

Smiler and Jan leave the hotel bar and walk up to their room. He rests one arm on her shoulder as they climb the spiral staircase and slips the other around her waist. She leans back against his chest. They giggle together, both a bit tipsy from wine and light-headed with anticipation.

Going into the room, hanging the DO NOT DISTURB sign on the door, closing it, savouring the moment yet anxious not to let it slip past or spoil, drawing the curtains against the dark wooded grounds of the hotel, turning down the lights. The room warm, the bed wide, their naked bodies together under the covers, the mattress creaking as they shift and curl closer into each other, slowly, with caution, touching.

And then he rolls on to his back and stares at the ceiling.

'Christ, I don't believe it. Here we are. Our one night of passion and I can't keep my bloody mind off what might happen to the boys when she finds out about us.'

'It's OK.'

'What a letdown. Christ.'

'It's OK.'

'It's not. It's pathetic.'

71

'I was thinking about my kids too. But let's think about something else now.

But he couldn't and neither could she really and though they had another go at sex later on, they rushed at it, strained at it, the need to make it happen taking away from the pleasure. Afterward, lying awake for hours talking, trying to unravel the domestic knots which were tightening around them, the tangled mesh of family. If only there weren't so many other people in their lives to consider. Would there ever be any room for the two of them?

If it could have been sunny, warm on the open road, warm enough to roll down the windows and feel the breeze on her bare arms as she sped along, Tina Turner on the cassette recorder belting out What's Love Got to Do With It – a song they both liked in spite of or maybe because of its title. Listening to the music, looking and feeling young, carefree. They'd meet at an idyllic and secluded spot on the coast, far away from the pit bings and the mills, and from there on everything would just slip into place as neatly as a well-folded bed.

Jan is driving more slowly than usual because the morning mist has thickened into a dense sea haar, hanging over the land like a pall, cutting visibility to a few yards. She has her fog lights on, but even so, the familiar road has become strange and treacherous, verging sharply to left and right, dipping and climbing into nothing. She narrowly misses a sheep, its yellow eyes two bright holes in the grey palpable air. With no landmarks visible, she loses sense of how far she has driven and almost misses the turn-off to the Safeways car-park.

She drives around until she finds Smiler's car then pulls up next to it. She switches off the engine. Smiler moves across to the passenger seat of his vehicle and rolls down the window. She rolls down hers. He takes her hands off the wheel, white-knuckled but otherwise red-raw from the laundry detergents. She's remembered to put on some hand-cream but it doesn't make a lot of difference. He's cleaned himself up, combed his hair but there's still confectioner's sugar in his fingernails.

They sit for a time like this, their hands clasped through the open windows, both of them glancing around at the sound of an approaching vehicle. The fog has one advantage. It creates the impression of being secluded even though they are surrounded by cars and shoppers. When they finally decide that nobody could identify them through the fog and when he invites her into his heated car for the last few minutes of their date, when they are together, she warming her hands in his as they sit in their swirling grey cocoon, it seems almost romantic.

MAGNOLIA

FOR SALE: Spacious ground floor flat.
Central location. Accommodation comprises
living room, kitchen/dining room, two
bedrooms, bathroom w. shower. Ample
storage. Extras.

OFFERS OVER: £35,000.

For further particulars and arrangements
to view, apply to the subscribers with whom
offers to be lodged.

GRUBB, GRACE & SNELL
Solicitors

The tenement flat was set back a few feet from the
pavement, behind a flimsy fence and some earth.
Puncturing the earth were the stumps of rose bushes
and a small leafless tree, a tree occupying one corner of
the plot between pavement and wall. Late November.
The earth hard. Nothing growing.

74

Inside it was everything they needed and more. They were in no doubt that it was the best they had seen and put in an offer as soon as they could contact their solicitor, a generous offer, generous enough to secure the sale.

They moved in. It seemed empty, a little bare in comparison to the cosy intimacy of the old place – though while they'd lived in it, it had felt cramped and cluttered, more of a transit camp than a real home. Now there was so much space to inhabit. They could stride through the hallway, stretch their arms wide and spin round without scraping their fingers against the walls. This was a place where they could stay a while, take time to fix up just as they wanted, a place where they would repair the loose windowframes, the cracks in the plaster, a place where they could put down roots.

In the conditions of sale, the sellers had made only one stipulation – that they could remove the tree from the patch of earth which was too small to be called a garden. Signing the deeds, the buyers readily agreed. The tree was nothing special to look at, not more at that time than a few ordinary leaves on a stunted trunk. They wondered, Did it have sentimental value? Had the people planted it when they first took on the place? The sellers couldn't take it immediately and requested that they might uproot it in the spring, after the flowering. The buyers instructed their solicitor to agree to the arrangement and promptly forgot about the tree.

After a slow dark winter, spring finally arrived and the few feet of earth between wall and pavement responded. All the usual seasonal flora began to force its way through the hard earth – demure snowdrops, cheery crocuses, brazen daffs and tulips. The creeper crept further up the masonry and, a little later, the tree blossomed.

That was when they began to notice it, the tree which turned out to be a magnolia – rare in such northerly parts – a tree bending under the weight of its blooms like a bridesmaid sinking into a curtsey. By day its creamy pink petals unfolded, by night its heady scent drifted through the open window. A Southern Belle on a plain Edinburgh street.

During the days which followed, passers-by often stopped at the gate to admire the tree, to discover its name, sometimes even to ask – if it wasn't being too cheeky – for a cutting. All the attention generated an interest from the householders. They began to take pride in the tree, observing it with the self-satisfaction of parents who had produced a beautiful daughter. They began to tend it, watering the roots regularly, inspecting the condition of the bark, the leaves, for blemishes and flaws about which they could worry and seek out remedies. The tree entered the routine of their lives. It entered their daydreams, transplanting them in distant, warmer climes. America, the Deep South.

One fine afternoon an elderly woman, leaning heavily on her stick, stopped at the gate. Her cloud of grey hair, her bloodless complexion, clawlike hands were in shocking contrast to the vibrant tree she admired. When she didn't move on, the woman of the house – who was sunning herself on the doorstep – began to explain that the tree's occupation of her garden – she now felt justified in naming it so – was limited, that it was due to be dug up in the near future.

The stranger shifted her gaze from the tree to its keeper. With the far-off look of death in her eyes, the look of seeing beyond the gaudy garden, the sturdy figure of the sunbather, the solid walls of the tenement behind which the constructions of the city stretched for miles – she grieved over the fate of the magnolia.

'It may never bloom again,' she said. 'My peonies, I tore them from their beds. They didn't like it. They pine for familiar soil. It's the same with magnolias.' The woman turned on her stick. 'I may not live to see my peonies bloom again.'

They have tightened windowframes, filled up cracks in the plaster. They have placed on mantelpieces, walls, shelves, windowledges, all their knick-knacks, potted plants, books, mirrors, paintings. They have taken up every inch of the place with the trappings of their life together. They are allowing the dust to settle and considering starting a family. They have grown accustomed to parting the curtains of an evening, gazing at the pale magnolia petals glowing in the moonlight as they listen to Billie Holiday singing of love and lynchings in the Deep South. They are at home. Home is a ground floor flat with a magnolia tree outside the living-room window. They have signed away their tree and now are loath to let it go. They have compiled a list of reasons to present – when the time comes – to the previous owners, reasons why the tree ought to remain in familiar soil, reasons quite independent of their own affection for it.

Meanwhile the tree continues to put forth new blooms. Its roots push deep and wide, into the foundations of the house, under the pavement, taking up all the space they can find.

SELF-PORTRAIT, LAUGHING

THE DAY TOM FISHER DIED, THINGS began to look up. First of all his wife Nora, from whom he had been estranged for a number of years – though they still shared the facilities – was overcome with guilt, sorrow and other associated emotions and changed overnight from a contemptuous and faithless wife into a penitent widow, instantly breaking off with Spender, her current lover.

The funeral party was small, mainly consisting of family. In later years Tom had become reclusive, spending most of his waking hours in the studio-cum-workshop he had hammered on to the sagging gable wall of the house. He had given up painting some years before his death and the studio had regularly been turned upside-down to accommodate new obsessions. Like a child learning to climb stairs, Tom immersed himself wholeheartedly in any new interest. When he tired of it, he wholeheartedly dropped it. Art, Tom would declare loudly – when his daughter Hazel returned home from design college with her dirty washing and an armful of books on Post-Expressionism – was old hat. As a subject of conversation in the Fisher household, art was forcibly dropped, in spite of Hazel's repeated attempts to interest her father in exhibitions she had seen down south.

For Tom, DIY initially replaced painting. Nora found herself coming home from work to an eager handyman, who sought jobs that needed doing and when there were none, invented some for himself. All this pleased Nora until her husband made a few mistakes, ruining some pieces of perfectly good furniture in the process. Later he turned to modelmaking, but found by this time that he had neither the patience nor, any longer, the dexterity. In his later years he settled for beermaking, which he discovered he could do easily and with an observable measure of success.

The Fisher home on the hot, airless day of the funeral reeked of hops and Uncle Dougie couldn't take his mind off a cool glass of beer when he discovered there was home-brew on the far side of the french windows. He proposed to Nora that the mourners drank a toast to Tom's memory, with the man's own beer.

Following Uncle Dougie's lead – and with Nora's nodded approval – the party moved through the french windows into Tom's workshop. It was at this point that Hazel, who had flown up from London that morning, gave way to tears at the sight of her father's canvases acting as sop trays for binfuls of fermenting hops. The workshop was like a potted history of her father's life. In the foreground, on the work-bench stood jars, tubes, thermometers, bottles. Behind these, pushed back carelessly, stood a doll's house, minus its roof, and a model tank lacking weaponry. Down the back of the bench were saws, drills, tubs of various sticky materials, sheets of plywood, strips of brass and steel, jam-jars full of nails and screws of every size. And from an even earlier time, stacked against every available wall, piled face-down on the floor, caked in dust and grime, were the remainder of the paintings.

Standing awkwardly amidst the clutter of the dead man's life, sipping with sad pleasure the dead man's very palatable beer, Uncle Dougie called the mourners to attention.

'I feel I must take it upon myself to say a word or two about my departed brother. We are gathered here now in the place Tom felt most at home, his place of work. And you can all see just by looking around you what kind of a man he was. Multi-talented, industrious to the last, with that extra special quality – self-motivation. Tom wasn't a man like the rest of us who need to be goaded into work, no, not Tom. Tom was the exception, pushing himself onwards.'

There was muted assent and some clearing of throats.

'I know it's a good number of years now since Tom has put paint to brush – in the artistic sense – but the man never stopped being creative. This very beer is the work of Tom's hand, and very good it is too. Now we all know Tom wouldn't like to be remembered simply as a brewer – though to my mind a man who can brew a good pint has a lot to recommend himself. I'm no artist myself, as most of you know, but you don't need to be a painter to recognise art when you see it and I'd say, as I'm sure everyone here would, that Tom Fisher was as good a painter as you'd find anywhere. And deserved a lot more recognition, not to mention reward, than was given him.'

Dougie would have continued but by this time Hazel

was sobbing loudly and Nora, with the frozen gaze of a sleep-walker, was approaching with a jug of beer. He had set the ball rolling, that was the main thing and by the time everyone left, the dead man's reputation among family and friends – as a prickly, bitter recluse – had been considerably revised.

For Nora, life with Tom had been an insecure business. A painter who had some talent but little public success was not the most consistent person to spend one's life with and Nora, though initially attracted to her husband's eccentricities, tired of the perennial lean times in his career. Tom had been a single-minded man, prepared to go without. Nora, once the child was on the way, was not. The novelty of being an artist's wife wore off. The lack of a regular income, her husband's see-sawing moods, the demands of a young child, rapidly turned romance into grind and Nora, who had always hoped for more, became deeply discontented with less.

When Hazel was settled in at school, Nora went out to work again, as a librarian in a city college. She had plenty of contact with students and staff and it wasn't long before she began looking at men with the open, inviting glance which read *available*. Where other women turn to a lover for thrills, Nora sought creature comforts, security, routine. A steady man with a steady, well-paying job was her idea of adultery and the college was an ideal location for meeting such men. There were frequent social events, brittle little affairs jollied up by dubious jokes, over-hearty laughter, an abundance of cheap wine and a communal need for something interesting to happen.

Tom Fisher wasn't a man who was prone to jealousy. Nor was he one who wanted to face the truth. When he first began to sense that he was losing Nora he buried himself in his painting with more vigour than usual, exhausting himself each day on his barely profitable work. His paintings, instead of becoming gloomy, became filled with light. He covered his canvases with bright, bold colours and strong, sensual curves. In this period of his life, the duration of his wife's first affair, he did his best work and was encouraged to exhibit.

Tom's one and only one-man show during his lifetime, though praised by the few painter friends he still kept up with at that time, didn't go down well with the critics. The reviews ranged from tepid to frosty and Tom was devastated by the adverse criticism. Outwardly he laughed it off but inwardly a light seemed to go out. He couldn't work. He fought with his daughter. He couldn't make love to his wife. This was quite the worst period of his life: unable to paint, unable to communicate with his family, unable to see a way forward.

Hazel could only spare a few days away from her studio to help her mother sort out Tom's belongings. Her father's death had come right in the middle of her first big commission – to design the interior of a new gallery near Covent Garden. Hazel had inherited her father's love of the visual and her mother's love of money and was determined to succeed where they had failed. She was energetic, independent and ambitious, her hard clear youthful eyes set on the summit.

Nora was in shock. Her movements were stiff, slow,

unnaturally feeble. She wandered through the house, picking up objects and replacing them, her husband's pipe, his beer mug, his battered jacket. The jacket had moulded itself over the years to fit the crook of his arm, the shrug of his shoulders. Hanging there, in the hall cupboard, his body still seemed to fill it. Nora lifted it off the hook and dropped it casually on the floor. Hazel took charge of her mother when Nora casually dropped a large clay fruit-bowl on the flagstones. Tom – in the brief phase when he attempted to become a potter – had made a range of bowls for Nora. This had been his own personal favourite, a coilpot, in the pit of which writhed glazed green snakes.

Hazel swept up the pieces of the broken bowl, sat her mother down and put a mug of tea in her hand. The mug said MUM on the rim and was another remnant from Tom's pottery days. Nora eyed the mug strangely, as if she might let it also smash on the floor. Hazel wrote out a list of Tom's belongings. As she went through it item by item, Nora scarcely commented. Tom's clothes were to go to the Salvation Army. His tools were to be given to Uncle Dougie's boy who was a mechanic and might find a use for them. Everything else was to go.

'Even the paintings?'

'Especially the paintings.' Hazel looked up from the piece of paper where she was taking notes. 'They won't fetch anything,' said Nora. 'Nobody knows the name anymore.'

'Maybe you should wait a bit before you make a decision. It's a big part of dad you'd be throwing away.'

'It's not a part of him I want to keep,' Nora replied.

Hazel herself had not been a great admirer of her father's

work. By the time she was a teenager Tom's paintings had degenerated into bland landscapes and wildly flattering portraits of neighbours' children. With the idealism – and insensitivity – of youth, Hazel accused him of selling out in favour of some quick money. They had argued fiercely about it but they had argued about everything then. Later they reached a silent, suspicious truce. Now, sitting at the kitchen table where she had sat as a child, drawing the insides of shells and slinky fashionable women, Hazel wished her father was out there in the workshop, so she could tap on the door and ask if he wanted yet another cup of strong sweet tea, wished she could make it up to him, make her peace.

'I'll deal with the paintings,' she said.

Once the house had been cleared, Hazel hired a small van, stacked the salvageable paintings in the back and drove to London, leaving her mother dazed but strangely contented.

For several months her father's paintings lay in her studio flat while she completed her work for the gallery. In spare moments, as a break from her own detailed plans, she would glance at them. She did not expect to be drawn again and again to the dusty, neglected canvases.

When the gallery was opened, Hazel's own work was highly praised and her reputation as a designer established. More work was immediately offered to her but, to her associates' surprise, she turned it down. With the money she had made on her last commission, she had her father's paintings cleaned, restored and framed. She took photographs, compiled a portfolio and sent it to the gallery, asking for exhibition space.

After the usual delays and in spite of some members of the selection board being dubious about presenting a recently deceased, unknown painter, her father's retrospective was – with Hazel's name adding weight to the application – eventually passed by the committee. Hazel arranged for invitations to be sent out.

Since Tom's death, Nora rarely went out. She had given up her job at the college library and gone into voluntary seclusion, passing her days in muted mourning, paying her respects to her late husband in the way she thought fit: she cleaned and cleaned, kept the windows open day and night. The last traces of Tom to leave the house were the smell of his beer and a lingering, but now faint whiff of turps. After nearly a year, the house smelled of nothing more than Muguet air-freshener. Nora had removed everything of her husband the better to remember him, to remember him uncluttered by the smelly, messy trappings of his life. The process of cleaning and airing had revived her but now there was nothing to do but sit in a bland, tidy house with nothing on the walls but clocks and calendars. Time began to weigh heavily on Nora and she began to find it impossible in this now ordinary, impersonal house, to imagine her husband at all.

Nora arrived late for the private view, missing the introductory words from the gallery manager and '*An Appreciation*', as Hazel's talk was described on posters which began at the tube station and stretched the length of the street.

With a catalogue clutched in her hand she edged around the gallery. The paintings, which for so long had been dust and expense – how she had bemoaned going without small personal luxuries for the sake of his stinking turps – were hardly recognisable to her, though most had adorned or, as she had said on occasion, *defaced* the walls of her house at one time or another. She stopped in front of a self-portrait she could not remember ever seeing before. The features were undoubtedly his but the expression – eyes bright slits, head thrown back in maniacal glee – was new to her. New and disturbing. The eyes seemed to follow her as she moved round the walls, as she stared in incomprehension at the paintings, as the laughing voice of her husband – so rarely heard in his lifetime – echoed in her ears. All around Nora slick, sleek people were chattering about the exhibition. Several of the paintings had red 'sold' stickers on them. Nora checked the price list. The figures were wildly high. Dead, Tom Fisher had found the ally close to so many unfortunate hearts: posterity.

THE ORIGINAL VERSION

ONCE UPON A TIME TWO WOMEN, Heather and Judy, become friends. They make arrangements – as their paths cross only through their children – to meet from time to time, thereby continuing and extending that friendship. Their meetings fall into three groups: trips with the children (two apiece, of similar age), dinners at each other's homes (husbands included) and nights out together. The first type of meeting takes them on picnics, trips to the park, the swimming pool, the museum, the beach. They fetch balls and wipe up spills, rarely finish a sentence or a cup of coffee. Then there are the dinners. These are occasions when the women tend to sit back and listen – through weariness or laziness rather than politeness – as their men make clumsy attempts to converse, tapping one subject and then another in search of a common chord, a conversational note on which to hang, a subject to sustain.

On nights out together they choose noisy, young people's bars, where the music is brash and the crowd animated. They want to be where the action is, without being a part of it. Occasionally one will point out a good-looking lad to the other and they'll giggle like schoolgirls.

Otherwise, they reminisce, speculate, gossip, tell each other secrets. These sorties are so rare, so fleeting, that confidences of one kind and another come tumbling out, prefixed by, *You're the first person I've told*, or *You'll never believe this*, or *I don't know if I should tell you* – the embarrassing, shocking, hilarious, the elating, the shameful, the excruciating. There's just time to hear the band play one more number, just time to finish a last drink before it's time to get back for the husband or the babysitter, and neither wants to go home just yet, there's more to tell but tomorrow will come round too soon as it is.

Secrets. Those private chips of information which have to be – on occasion, under restricted circumstances – tested in the world, like newly discovered chemicals. What effect will a certain piece of information have on the friend whom you have made part of your own personal experiment? Or rather, how will it react with that chosen friend? If you carry secrets, you also carry doubt, yet that doubt, that need to take a risk, to expose some hidden chunk of yourself to another, is the point on which many friendships rest. In early childhood, telling someone a secret was a true mark of friendship. Not just a mark but the quintessential test of that friendship. Give away the secret you have been told and you lose a friend. Perhaps you make another friend in the process but the new bond is tainted by betrayal.

Of the two friends in this story, Heather – as well as some home typing and proof-reading for a small publishing house – writes her own stories, which occasionally appear in magazines. At first Heather keeps this activity of hers secret from Judy. She has noticed in the past that some people, on hearing what she does in her spare time, tend to become reticent and suspicious, as if what she did was tantamount to spying, as if, as soon as she had left a person's company, she would rush home and take detailed notes on the occasion – what had been said and done, as well as some descriptive detail useful for conjuring up the atmosphere of the said occasion. In fact she has never taken such notes. Except this once.

It was a case of trading secrets. Late one night the pair of them had been gossiping about their partners, as everyone does from time to time. They got on to 'the worst moments of marriage'. Judy told Heather about a time – one of many – when she and her husband Jimmy had almost split up. She put everything into the narration: she rolled her eyes, paused meaningfully, mimicked herself and her husband in such a way that Heather was clutching her sides with laughter one minute and open-mouthed in disbelief the next.

Jimmy was a photographer, covering weddings, babies and houses for sale. It wasn't a great living but with people marrying and babies being born and houses being bought and sold on a regular basis, there was plenty of work. Around the time Judy gave birth to their second child, Jimmy ventured into a new field, 'boudoir photography', which basically meant soft porn shots (tastefully sensual compositions) of a man's wife or girlfriend, intended for private consumption on the bedroom wall. The golf club secretary – who was commissioning the work – had a long list of interested members and was offering a considerably higher fee per portrait than was usual for brides or babies.

The story of Judy and Jimmy was a familiar enough case

of a clash of attitudes. She was opposed to him taking on 'that kind of work'. He argued that it was a harmless enterprise – wasn't it better a man had his wife's photo on the wall than a pile of magazines under the bed? Besides, they were short of money at the time and beggars couldn't be choosers.

Days, weeks later, Heather found that this story, in particular its ending, became lodged in her mind. The image of her friend burning her husband's entire series of 'boudoir portraits' on the compost heap kept resurfacing in her mind, demanding attention. She found herself playing around with the facts, noting down phrases and details from what she could remember of Judy's story. She couldn't stop herself twisting the facts towards fiction.

The next time she met Judy, Heather let her 'secret' occupation be known. As Judy's reaction was one of inter-est and enthusiasm, she went on to say that she'd been thinking a lot about the boudoir photos and wanted to write a story based on them. It would be quite differ-ent from the original version. Names, of course, would be changed. And other personal details. She would not expose her friend's private life in print. She would not give away her secret. Judy, rather than raising any objec-tions, glowed with bashful pride and volunteered more information.

Heather began work on the story. It took longer to complete than she had anticipated. Her children were ill in succession, her husband was working away from home a lot. And the story became longer and more complex than she had anticipated. The closing scene, in particular, took many drafts to perfect. Like the coy poses of golfing wives veiled by bonfire smoke, it became strangely hazy, suggestive rather than sharply defined.

By the time the piece was ready to show Judy – who insisted on seeing the final draft – the other's life had improved. Changes at home. A couple of jobs to try for. She had new stories of her own to tell and felt no urgency to read Heather's version of an episode from her life. The whole scenario was much less important to Judy now than it was to Heather.

When the two women next meet it is at Heather's flat. There is the unnatural hush which occurs just after a young child has fallen asleep. The two of them tiptoe in from the door, slide chairs up to the coal fire, uncork the wine gingerly, set down tumblers as if they were fine crystal. It's less of an occasion than going out together.

'I read your story,' Judy says, after they have caught up on each other's news. She pauses just long enough for Heather to doubt the whole enterprise and sense a sickening flutter of panic.

'I liked it,' Judy adds with a smile. Relieved, Heather also smiles, briefly mentions a few difficulties she had and changes she made, then steers the conversation back to gossip. The two of them are soon blethering away just as if they were out on the town, until the whimper of a stirring child cuts the conversation abruptly. When no more crying follows, they resume their talk, in voices which are subdued, intimate.

'But you shouldn't believe everything I say,' says Judy. 'Jimmy's not as bad as you've made him out to be. I still love him, from time to time.'

Heather emphasises that the character of Dick was never intended to be a portrait of Judy's husband, that she had gone out of her way to make him different from Jimmy. 'Except for a couple of details.'

'But walking the dog, that's Jimmy, and the steam baths . . .'

'That's all. Just a couple of details.'

'And the way the woman Jeanette behaved. She was too calm, too composed about it all. It wasn't like that. I was wild. Out of control. I made a scene.'

Judy continues, tongue loosened by the wine, retelling her original version, embellishing as she goes.

And so it becomes apparent, after all, that Judy likes the story but prefers her own version, the original, the truth, and although Heather insists that her version is truth of a kind, that it is composed of real elements, as she is saying all this, as she is defending herself, the feeling comes over her that, instead of making a small idea grow large, the process has reversed, that the story which she spent much time coaxing into existence, is now shrinking into invisibility. Her friend seems to have so much more to say in her impromptu ramble than she with her tidy, revised paragraphs.

'What about the ending?' says Heather, eventually.

'The ending?'

'Of the story. The bonfire.'

'Oh that! That was really good. I could just picture the woman Jeanette standing there with the tongs in her hand, eyes lit up like a madwoman as each photo curled up at the edges before it caught fire, like a kind of slow torture. And the husband's look of constipated rage. I liked that.'

'Because it matched up to the truth?'

'Well, the thing is, that bit about the bonfire . . . it didn't really happen like that.'

'I see,' says Heather quietly, miserably. 'Maybe writing another version wasn't such a good idea.'

'No,' says Judy. 'What I mean about the ending is, it never happened. I made it up. While I was telling you the story I got carried away and added an ending. It was what I felt like doing, but all I really did was rip up a couple of dud prints, rejects, and chuck them on with the grass cuttings. I should have burnt the lot. Definitely the right ending. Truth or fiction. What's so funny?'

When Heather finally stops laughing they finish off the bottle between them. The fire is dying down and in the embers, they both imagine the crackling, sizzling soft porn bonfire, and they share a silence full of secrets.

LANDA OPPORTUNITY

NO KIDDIN! PSYCHOLOGY MAJOR? MY KID brother's a shrink. Up in Boston. Me, I'm more the philosopher – self-taught – the freelance observer of my fellow man, woman, kid, dog – always on the look-out for life's basic ingredients. Which is why my brother's filthy rich and I'm clean broke. But me, I got imagination, whereas my brother, he don't even know how to dream without all kindsa deep meaning messin up the action. Dreams, he tells his patients – at around ten bucks a word – are where it's at. But mostly, I reckon, my brother dreams about bucks, big bucks, thousand dollar bills swirling about on the sidewalk like food wrappers, drifting inta the trash-can which – pity it only happens in dreams – turns inta the night-deposit chute at the bank. That's where my brother goes nights – the goddamn bank – once his patients have dumped their dreams inta his dictaphone.

Wanna try one of my meatballs? I need a second opinion.

So I guess you'll quit waitressin at the enda the summer? Back ta school in the fall? College must be a lotta fun. I never did bother with it myself – my kid brother's fees ate up our parents' savings – but I'll bet all that studying pays off. That's one thing you can still say for this country, you can go places with an education. Doesn't matter who you are or where you're comin from – the highway to the top is straight ahead. Yep, one thing's for sure, this is still the landa opportunity, and don't let anyone tell you different.

Landa opportunity. Landa power. That's my kid brother's trip, power. He gets off on playing God to psychs. Who wouldn't, if you reckon up the leisure time. Short days in the consulting suite and long weekends on the sailboat with his shrink wife. That's the only catch, the wife. That dame's close to the brink herself. Crazy shrink bitch. Excuse me, but really, she's the kind who'd throw herself overboard if ya looked at her the wrong way. Like you tell her you dig her outfit, she gets mad at you. Shit, I mean, what kinda reaction is that? I mean, why wear a dress that looks like cling-wrap if you don't wanna be noticed?

But I tell ya, I'm not so crazy about my brother's lifestyle. Nor his wifestyle. No friggin way do I covet my brother's wifestyle. Don't get me wrong, I don't say every dame in the brain business is looped out. You sure don't look like you fit that bill.

So whatd'ya reckon? Does my sauce need a drop more love and affection? Or maybe a dasha the spice a life? My taste buds are dead. I can always tell a Saturday. By Happy Hour I can't taste a friggin thing but garlic. I ask myself, why bother with hors-d'oeuvres? The jerks we get in here for Happy Hour just suck them up three at a time and don't give a shit what they're eatin so long as they don't haveta pay. Not one a these guys knows howta savour a thing. It gets to me, this place. You take a buncha trouble ta get the flavour spot on. It figures you'd appreciate some kinda acknowledgement for improvin on potato chips, right? But all that crummy bunch out there see is somethin to soak up their beer between lunch and dinner. A little appreciation is all I need.

My kid brother doesn't need appreciation. If his clients don't dig his analysis, they sue, so if they leave his office without a scene, he's happy. Goes home to his deep, big buck dreams. Shit, I gotta get outta here. A guy's gotta have a whole buncha imagination to stick around in this clapboard acropolis. It's OK for a young person like you, I guess, and anyway you've got school ta get back ta, but for a guy like me, it's really the pits. I mean, they hire me ta cook Greek and then what? They ration the friggin olive oil. I gotta substitute corn oil and low-grade corn oil at that. Olive oil, corn oil, jeez, it's like givin a guy water and askin him ta turn it inta wine. Lemme tell ya, I'm an inventive guy but some things ya just can't fake. Jeez, they hire me ta bring up this joint from the third-rate liquor hole it's turned inta since Benny hit the rye and Stavros got dropped from the Fall River Flyers. I tell ya, I perform miracles in this goddamn kitchen.

I gotta give ya a piece a advice, babe. Watch out for Stavros. He's one horny motherfucker when he's lit, which is most nights around the time you girls knock off, know what I mean? Benny, now Benny's a different ball game. He won't try nothing like that but he can be real mean. I mean really. Last waitress he hired quit on her first night. She screwed up on a coupla orders and Benny wouldn't lay off bustin her ass about it. So look out for yourself, babe. And watch out for the brothers Constantinos.

97

So what makes a good-lookin lady like you go in for pokin inta folks' brains? Typa women in the psych world – I gotta be frank about this, I mean they're so friggin extreme. Ya got frigids, ya got nymphos and not a whole lot in between. And eating disorders – stuffin and starvin. That kinda thing sure is no recipe for a good time. I mean, I'm the kinda guy who likes to cook dinner for a date, give her a tasta my style. But with a woman like that, what happens? Ya get the place all set for a neat little love feast – candles, flowers – me, I go for tiger orchids, they sure beat roses for sexiness. Ya sit the lady down to an aperitif – I have the best recipe for screwdrivers ya'll ever taste in your life. Ya bring on the food and the next thing ya know your date's tellin ya she can't touch a forkful of any friggin dish ya fixed. Or ya get the other type who homes in on her plate and eats until she has to excuse herself and go throw up in the washroom.

For me, a woman should be like a good steak, medium rare. No way do I go for overdone – steak or dames. Some sauce, maybe. I like a little sauce.

Go easy on the mayo, will ya? That tub's gotta last the night.

My brother, he always had a tough time with dames. One would check him out – he always had looks on his side – they'd date. She'd find out he was a shrink and the next thing ya know she's thinkin, I'm a real screwed-up person. Right now, I don't need romance. I don't need sex. Right now, what I need is analysis. Here's a guy who can supply it for free so I'm gonna go for it. So my brother gets himself all tied up in sortin out her head and misses out on any kinda fun. Me, I may be a little past my prime – know what they say – used to be a Greek god, now just a goddamn Greek – but I've still got an appetite for a tasty lady.

No way would I trade places with my kid brother. Sure, I wouldn't say no to his padded cell. Ten rooms, five acres and half a lake. Way up in the mountains. Plus a condo in downtown Boston.

Hot plates! Use your napkin if you don't want blistered fingers. Now remember, it's Saturday night. You got no timeta hang about shootin the breeze. I need those orders in double quick. We're gonna be busy busy. Sure is a bad night to begin but make it through tonight and you'll make out okay in tips.

What's this you're givin me? Another order for steak? What's with these guys? They go eat Greek, then order a friggin steak. I got two trays of pastitio to clear tonight. You girls are gonna haveta push the pastitio, right?

Jeez, I been here way too long, workin my butt off for these cheapos. I gotta keep tellin myself, Nico, you're a smart guy, you can rise above this shit. Hang in there, make your stack then get the hell out. I'd get a better job in the city. Any goddamn day. Been thinkin about movin up to Boston. I could hang out at my brother's place until I got set up. Except that crazy wife of his would drive me nuts. One thing's for sure, I won't be wastin my talents in this joint much longer. Right now, I'm gettin psyched for a shift and lemme tell ya, the next move I make's gonna be the big one.

The way I see life, it's having collateral that counts. You can grab a hold of collateral. My brother and his buddies, they got it wrong. All that psychobabble about attitude.

Money in the bank is where it's at – and a warm woman on your arm.

Day off tomorrow. You too, right? Gonna fix me a late, late breakfast and just laze the day away. Maybe take a drive by the beach. Ya like the beach? Take it or leave it? But, hey, ya should get down there and tan up while the weather holds. Lemme tell ya, nothin lasts forever.

Say, ya know what? I just had a great idea. Ya're new in town, right? Don't know your way around? Why don'tcha lemme show ya the sights? I know this town like I know my apartment – too goddamn well. My apartment's neat and real cosy. Tiny, maybe, but it's got class. I don't deal with shoddy goods, unless, like here, I got no option. But one place ya gotta see around here is Ocean Drive. Ten miles of pure money. Makes me green as hell but I love it all the same. When I'm real low I go take a drive out there and remind myself I'm in the landa opportunity. And a citizen of that land. Nobody can turn me out. Those mansions on Ocean Drive are wild. Like, everyone's got their vision of what they'd build if they hit the big-time but these guys did it. Who knows, maybe a coupla them started out skewering souvlaki. All kindsa movies've been shot in the mansions.

We could drive around a while, take in a few aperitifs, then go back to my place for dinner. I got some tenderloin just beggin to be smothered in mushrooms à la Greque.

Whatd'ya say? Gonna give it a whirl?

Table Four ready to go. Gimme your answer later, okay?

I get the picture, sure. Ya gotta study. Even on vacation ya gotta study. Ya got such a tight schedule ya can't spare one Sunday, right? Sure, I believe ya, but don'tcha reckon a break for a day might be fun? I mean, all work and no play . . . but I'm a philosophical guy, like I told ya . . . at least ya didn't say ya had ta wash your hair. I can handle a knockback. That's somethin a guy like me gets to be real good at, a guy like me who hasn't a lot going for himself in the first place. But all I'm sayin is, it's too bad ya wanna pass up a good time.

Don't reckon ya'd miss much? Listen, babe, I got no shortage a lady friends. No way would ya be doin me any kinda favour by comin along for the ride. I gotta whole lista lady friends. Wanna see my telephone book?

My attitude? Whatd'ya mean attitude? I wasn't aimin on comin on heavy, I mean, I just had it in my mind – as you're new and all – to show ya some hospitality. Shit, you psychs are all the same, tyin your friggin brains in knots. I tell ya, babe, you're beginnin ta sound like ya really need a night out.

Hey! Get back here. Just where d'ya plan on headin with my souvlaki dinners lookin like that. Ya bring that order right back here, d'ya hear me? Garnish, babe, ya hearda garnish? Ever done this kinda work before? Too busy book readin for the real worlda work? Look – lettuce here, half tomato here, coupla slices cuke on the side, chunka lemon sittin on the lettuce. Always lemon with souvlaki. Shit, the things folks don't know. Forget the lemon and you lose the friggin flavour. Besides, ya gotta pretty up the dish, see? Dress that naked meat. Ya do it for yourself, right? Ya try ta show yourself ta advantage? When ya serve the food, my food, ya give it some presentation.

Psych women, shit. I clean forgot about depressives.

How could I forget about depressives. Ya must be that type. I thought there was somethin weird about ya. Folks who go in for psych always got some kinda personal problems. Depressives are the worst. Hell to live with. I should know. My second wife was one. Pure neat hell. Was I relieved when she packed her bags. I mean, my first wife got crazy now and again, like if I quit my job or blew the rent at the bar. She'd break a few plates around the house but she was okay. I knew where I was with my first wife. I always knew she'd go look somewhere else for a meal ticket. Didn't take her long, I tell ya. And then my second wife comes along and things go from stormy to friggin hurricane weather. Shit, I'm the kinda guy who wants an easy life, no heavy duty interaction.

Okay, move it now, move it. Food's gettin cold. Shift your ass out there. And try a friggin smile, babe. Nobody's gonna tip ya a red cent if ya don't quit scowling.

Ya know, maybe ya should give my kid brother a call. See if he can help ya out. In his professional capacity, I mean.

LITTLE BLACK LIES

HE'S ON THE EMPTY DANCE-FLOOR, alone with the spinning lights and the driving beat, doing what he does so well, making his body bend and sway to the rhythm of the song. The song's immaterial. He'll dance until he drops. He'll dance until the beat stops pounding in his head, the beat of the drum, of the ocean waves on the shore, of his mother's spade hitting the hard ground, of his unbroken heart.

Sonny K. Lee was brought to this coastal New England town, a bright-eyed black-skinned baby. His mother piled her five kids on to a Greyhound bus going north and stopped at Providence, Rhode Island. As she had no money to travel further, she hoped that, with a name like Providence, the Lord would provide.

After several months in a dirty city hostel, she and the children were allocated a house in Midtown, where she dug up the grass in the front yard and planted cabbage and potatoes. Midtown was not a town in itself but a cheap housing complex tagged on to the tail end of the handsome town of Freeport. The population of Midtown was mostly black, of Freeport itself, mostly white. Between welfare cheques, cleaning jobs in Freeport mansions, and later the eldest boy's wages from Speciality Pets, the family was fed, clothed, schooled and taken to church on Sundays.

The kids grew up and gradually left home. The eldest, Mikey, married a solid girl who cooked good cheap food, kept a clean house, and had the faith. At the pet store Mikey was promoted from birds to reptiles and got a line going in crocodiles. As a youngster, Sonny would go along on Saturdays, flatten his nose against the glass and eye the weird birds and beasts with fear and wonder.

All the kids worked out, the way Sonny told it. Tillie was wed soon after Mikey. Babies came quickly. She got big and laughed like she was happy. Nina stayed skinny, single, busy, distributing religious pamphlets and organising outings for old folks. Will was going steady.

Sonny as a teenager, restless, sees a movie about a young black dancer, gets it into his head that the movie is speaking directly to him, flies the coop for New York.

He moves in with Charles, who keeps him in Levis and Cool cigarettes and lusts after his young black body. Perhaps there is more to it than that. Sonny believes so. Love is mentioned from time to time. Charles is thirty-five, white, a café-owner with friends in New York who do things in the arts.

Sonny is found a place in dance school, which keeps him off the streets during the day and in adorable shape for Charles, who likes to show him off at parties.

Sonny in a white suit, high on champagne, flutters on Charles's arm, saying little, laughing a lot. Sonny, the well-behaved pet, plucks his master off the floor, takes him home when he's drunk too many cocktails.

His life with Charles didn't last. The older man tired of the social whirl – too many nights of idleness, too much wine – dried out in a detox ward, sold his café and opened a bookshop. Sonny had just found his wings, longed to stretch them, to be out in the world. Charles's appreciation wasn't enough. The inevitable arguments ensued, Sonny throwing his emotions around, Charles coolly backing off.

When Sonny's booking in the third-rate musical – which was all his dance training got him – packed up, was followed by a year of no work at all and a trail of loveless one-night stands, he quit New York and returned to his home town.

His sisters swooped on him with questions. What you been up to? You got a honey down there? How come you so skinny? His mother eyed him reproachfully and forced him to eat a plate of hot chilli. The prodigal had returned. The word got round and the entire family, plus wives, husbands and even more kids, showed up first thing Sunday morning dressed for church. The reunion was not a success. Sonny refused to attend the service.

When his mother came back from church, she told him calmly, that though it grieved her to say it, Sonny would have to find his own home. If he couldn't attend church, he must be some kind of sinner and she wouldn't have no sin in her house. He'd still be welcome for visits but had better not bring no wicked habits with him. Tillie and Nina tried to console him. Get yourself a girl, they said, and bring her home.

He got himself a job bartending at the Michelangelo, a

gay place on Prospect Hill, where they had disco music and dancing waiters. Sunday was the big day. While his mother was praying for his soul, Sonny stocked up the liquor shelves. What else could he do? Dancing, dressing up, drinks and men were what he knew. That had been his sentimental education. After Charles, though, there had been little sentiment involved. Was that what he came back for? Sentiment?

Though his mother didn't know the first thing about Sonny's life on the white side of town, his sisters kept tabs on him. Early on a Sunday morning, before Sonny had opened up, they'd slip into the bar to say Hi. Nina would bring her religious pamphlets and Tillie would bring hot doughnuts. Sonny made them coffee and made them laugh. They'd go away happy. They didn't ask too much about his life, just was he eating, was he having a good time, and where did he get those fine shoes?

Sonny was happy, happier than he'd been in New York, even with Charles. Here he wasn't just another poor boy, living on tips and invitations to dinner. He made his own living and his own friends. Sonny made friends without really trying. Having spent some years in the city and picked up some social skills, an extrovert style in clothes and a love of fun, he was in demand. He laughed loud and camped it up, sewed outfits to wear at work, rented a small apartment next door to the bar, and often entertained, after hours.

Although he was back more or less where he grew up, new doors were opened, old ones closed. In the black bars off West Broadway – the only black bars in town – folk like Sonny, whatever their colour, were not welcome. At first his life revolved around the Michelangelo. Men flocked to him, women too, even though for them there was never any question of a romantic or physical relationship.

As the years passed, Sonny gained a degree of acceptance in some of the town's fashionable restaurants where he entertained and overtipped. Also, largely due to Sonny's efforts, non-gays began to drop in to the Michelangelo. Some came only out of voyeuristic curiosity, some hoped for more, a few simply came for the dancing.

It is a clear fall Sunday and the bar stays quiet until late afternoon, when the light begins to fade. Guy, Sonny's young man of recent months, plays pin-ball until the place fills up. Guy is twenty, restless. Sonny is thirty-five.

Robert and Donna are seated at the bar. They've been coming the last few Sundays and there's no mistaking why they're here. Robert leaves Donna seated at the bar for long spells while he cruises the dance-floor. In idle moments Sonny chats to the woman. He doesn't like anyone to feel bad and she surely does, in spite of her smiles. The couple are British, over on vacation, planning to head west to California. They're not married but had been considering it, before Robert began to take more interest in the Michelangelo than in Donna.

Late in the evening and the bar is still busy. Sonny's on the dance-floor, taking a break from serving customers by entertaining them with an impromptu floor show. He spins the mirrored ball and leaps into the pool of coloured lights. Out of the corner of his eye he sees Guy necking with a blond boy, a boy his own age. It was bound to happen and now it has. And now things will change. Now Guy will find

Sonny old, will no longer admire him. History will repeat itself. Guy will find faults in Sonny, flaws. Love has not been mentioned between them for some time.

Sonny breaks off his dancing. There's trouble at the bar. The English guy is slapping his girl about the head. She's yelling at him to lay off. Sonny gently prises them apart. Robert is asked to leave. He attempts to drag Donna with him but Sonny prevents this happening. She'll see you when she's good and ready, he says. And not before. Robert screams abuse at Sonny as he leaves.

Sonny has just been to visit his mother. Her sight is failing. She's having trouble reading the hymn book. Them words keep dancing about and playing tricks on me, she says. I don't sing nothing I don't know by heart no more, lest I mess it up. Sonny is sympathetic. He has endless patience for the problems of others. For his own he has less time, less ability. Of his own he can tell his mother nothing. Guy has been messing him up lately, and there was the business with Donna.

She doesn't go with her pale English boyfriend to California. She turns up on Sonny's doorstep with a black eye and a visa about to expire. She wants to stay in town, get a job, but she's a foreigner and needs a permit. Sonny, without giving the matter much thought, offers to marry her. That way she would be a legal resident. There's no problem, he tells her. A marriage of convenience. People do it all the time. A wife on paper won't affect his life and apart from a blood-test and some forms to be signed, there's nothing to it. Donna, on reflection, gratefully accepts.

Everyone in Sonny's wide circle of friends gets to know

about the wedding. To some it's a great joke, to others a generous gesture. Guy is impressed by the outrageousness of it all, sees the occasion as a wonderful excuse for a party. Sonny's boss at the Michelangelo – where Sonny has worked for ten years – offers to pick up the tab for the party.

The day of the wedding is bright and clear. The maple in front of the Court House is golden. Sonny, Donna and their two witnesses – Guy and his sister – all dressed up and giggling wildly, enter the building. The registrar glances casually at the party and then looks again in disbelief. Sonny getting married!

Somehow Sonny hadn't expected a real ceremony, with real vows, and here he was, repeating them after the registrar with this girl he hardly knew. And when it came to saying the words, love, honour, cherish, he found he was saying them, not just as part of the arrangement they had agreed on. Saying the words, he was meaning them, feeling them. When asked to kiss the bride, he did so. He meant that too.

The party at the Michelangelo continued well into the night. When the guests had eventually gone home, Donna went to her bed and Sonny to his, with Guy.

As a result of the marriage several things happened. The first was that Sonny and his new wife began to be invited into homes where he had previously been unwelcome. It soon became obvious that his hosts believed that Sonny had gone straight for real. The second was that his sisters heard the news through a friend at the Court House and arrived the following Sunday. They ticked him off for not inviting them to the wedding, then hugged him and asked a hundred questions about his wife. And Ma says, Hurry and bring her home, now, Nina added, before she and Tillie rushed off to church.

Why didn't Sonny set the record straight? Was it because he couldn't bear those doors to be shut again to him, doors which had taken so long to open? Or was it his family? He hadn't intended them to know but they did and were, in spite of not being invited to the wedding, in spite of the girl being white and a foreigner, delighted about it.

Donna, a little uncomfortably, went along with Sonny's story. She felt she owed him this much. Also, they were spending a good deal of time together with all these double invitations. The husband and wife were becoming close friends. Donna helped Sonny pick himself up when his affair with Guy ended, sat with him as he talked late into the night about wanting to settle with someone steady.

This wasn't the Sonny everyone knew and enjoyed. How much did he mean what he said, how much was a hopeless wish to please everyone, especially his mother? Her health was poor. She hadn't the strength to turn the soil in her yard but she kept on toiling in that patch the Lord – via state welfare – had provided.

The time for coming clean about the whole affair passed, and, at Sonny's request, Donna agreed to meet his family. She even cooked dinner for them one evening at Sonny's apartment, giving his relations the impression that she lived there, reinforcing the unspoken lie. When they left, he turned to her. I want to make love to my wife, he said. Donna, thinking that her husband of convenience was taking the charade too far, lightly dismissed the request, said goodnight and went upstairs to her own apartment.

She hears him through her floor. He's out on the empty dance-floor, alone with the spinning lights and the driving beat, doing what he does so well, making his body bend and sway to the rhythm of the song. He'll dance until he drops, dance until the beat stops pounding in his head, the beat of the drum, of the ocean waves on the shore, of his mother's spade hitting the hard ground, of his unbroken heart.

THINGS AS THEY ARE

DOLORES LET HER GAZE SLIDE OFF the midday soap. Through the picture window, the one she'd had Tony's boys put in special, she watched as the crew spilled out of the truck and began to drag the net down from the back. Instinctively she patted her hair into place at the sight of them, in oil-smeared overalls and rubber boots, messing up her yard, stinking the place out. The smell of fish would hang around for hours after they'd quit fouling up her prize-winning view of the harbour.

They'd come one time, photographers, make-up artists, you name it, them newspaper folks fetched it right up to her home, the most distant spot from which the Bay of Galilee could be seen. Difference was, they'd cleaned up after them: she hadn't been left with slime and fishbone gumming up the tarmac, no, and she'd been presented with two framed photos of Tony's trawler steaming into harbour. You couldn't see Tony, of course, but who needed to see their husband in a photo if they'd been looking at him on and off – More off than on, Ma, Margie'd said before she upped and left for Martha's Vineyard – for twenty-five years.

Dolores padded across the carpet and opened the window.

'You boys! See and keep that there net off my lawn. Ain't not this minute done hosing it down.' Without waiting for a reply, she pulled the window to, but didn't close it entirely. Not that she'd ever been one for snooping, but you couldn't trust them boys to keep a clean mouth on them.

That day, though, it wasn't cussing which interrupted her favourite TV serial, but a laugh, an unmistakeably female laugh, which for sure didn't come from any of her shrill neighbours. She couldn't believe it at first, there sure was no way of reckoning by dress, but right in the middle of her own front yard, hauling on the net next to Philly the cook – there was no mistaking when she looked closely – was a female, pitching in just like a regular hand. Philly had a grin on his face as wide as a submarine sandwich.

'Capello!' Dolores yelled through the window. 'C'mere this minute!' Her short stout husband looked up gloomily. He drooped at the shoulders, sagged at the middle. 'You hear me?'

'I hear you, I hear you. Can't it wait, Dolores? Net's all busted up.' He waved his arm behind him – the fool – as if she of all folks needed to be shown what a torn net looked like.

'More'n a net'll need mending if you don't fetch yourself up here,' she threatened, prompting a low, scandalised whistle from Philly. Tony cast around for sympathy but the crew knew better than to interfere: every head was averted.

'Mind and keep them boots on the papers,' said Dolores,

hearing her husband's boots on the doormat. She pointed to her newsprint path across the gleaming kitchen floor but kept her eyes trained on the TV.

'Quite a sheen, Dolores,' he said. 'You sure do keep this place nice.'

'You and them boys sure do mess it up.'

'What is it, Dolores? I can't say what it is but you look different. Been at the hairdresser's this morning? Got yourself a new hairdo?'

'I don't believe,' she replied, 'that you've got time to stall, if you're planning on heading out tomorrow.'

Of course she'd been at the hairdresser's. Anyone could see that she'd just had her thin dry hair permed into a tight ball of curls. She always made an effort for Tony's last night ashore. First and last, she used to say to Margie, that's what sticks.

'I ain't blind,' she said. 'And don't act like you don't know what I mean. Tell me one thing. Since when did a female work boats?'

'Dolores,' he replied patiently, 'these are modern times. Why, girls do all kindsa things these days. Didn't Margie tell you herself that over in the Vineyard . . .'

'Don't talk to me about that place. What folks do over there don't make no difference round here. And don't talk to me about Margie. She ain't been home in six months.'

'Why don't you give her a call? No sense in fretting when you can just pick up the phone.'

'Ain't the same. You know it. And another thing you know's that there's only one kinda female job aboard – and it ain't nothing to do with catching fish.'

Dolores turned to face her husband. She stared at him

as though she expected to find guilt written all over him but he looked just the same as ever. Not much of a catch if looks were anything to go by, but he'd always been a good husband, by anyone's reckoning. She didn't know what a telltale sign might have been. How could she? Nothing of this kind had come up before. She'd always known near on every move her man made. He'd go to sea, come home fifteen, maybe twenty days later, drink for two days – she'd tolerate no more – then spend the next week muddling around the house, under her feet more often than not.

'Deck's no place for a woman. You always said so yourself. I've never even set foot on deck,' said Dolores. 'Not that nobody did ever invite me.' Tony stood shifting his weight from one foot to the other, marooned on his paper island. The house had always been Dolores's territory. After all, he was only at home one week in three, on average.

'Talk to her at lunch, Dolores. She's just a regular girl, like Margie,' he said, and returned to work.

Although she'd never literally set foot on deck, Dolores had inspected the boat from all possible vantage points. She'd peered through portholes: she knew to a cubby-hole what the inside was like. Two cabins – one for her husband (with spare berth) and the other for the rest of the crew. She could picture it: the skipper's cabin would be dimly lit, the polished brass lamps glowing, the gaslight flickering as the boat rocked gently, like a cradle. The moon would be shining directly on to the girl lying on the spare berth, two feet away from her husband. There would be a light slap of waves against the hull, her husband would stretch out an arm, or the girl would . . . but that was as far as it was decent to imagine. Dolores had always believed in knowing when to stop.

The net had been spread over the entire length of the driveway. The girl was at the far end, cross-legged, her head bent into her work, her long hair obscuring her face. Dolores became aware that the yard was unusually peaceful: no lewd jokes flew about: there was none of the familiar horseplay – in fact, there was nothing for her to complain about. It wasn't right. It was that girl's doing.

'It's a fine view you got here, Mrs Capello,' said the girl. The crew were nearly done with lunch, which until now, had been eaten in silence. Dolores had not taken a seat at the table that day, but had remained standing, inspecting each one of them, like a detective, for signs of complicity.

'Dolores,' said Tony. 'Girl's talking to ya.'

'Ain't hard of hearing,' she replied. 'Don't make no difference what I see or don't see. Ain't seeing what counts.'

'Hey, hey, Dolores,' Tony continued. 'How about some pickles? My wife makes terrific pickles,' he added, to no one in particular.

'Reckon you've enough spice in your life, Capello.' Philly sniggered into his sandwich. The girl laughed, just like Margie had done.

'I ain't never been one for cracking jokes,' said Dolores. 'And if you're all done filling your bellies I'll get this place shipshape again.'

It was early evening before the net was patched up and loaded on to the truck. Dolores was back at the window again. She'd been leafing through the family album – wedding photos, baby photos, Margie's first day at school, Christmases, birthdays, family vacations, Margie's graduation from high school. There were only two more of her daughter, one taken in that ramshackle apartment she rented at the Vineyard.

Margie had loved her pa when she was little. He'd given her everything she'd ever asked for; drives to Rocky Point, clam bakes, barbeques, fun of all kinds and what did she do? Turned her back on it all, for that crummy apartment. Why don't you get yourself a decent place to stay, in a smart neighbourhood, Dolores had said. Why do you have to go mixing with bums and crazy people? Margie had laughed herself sick.

Tony stood at the far end of the drive, talking to the girl. Dolores couldn't hear what was being said but she could see her husband pull his bill-fold from his back pocket. Crew weren't paid until a trip was over and the catch had been sold: Tony was paying the girl off. Satisfied, Dolores fetched the laundry and settled into ironing her man's shirts. He would drop off the crew, he'd come home, just like always, clean himself up. They'd have dinner, go for a drive perhaps. She'd have a cocktail, just one, he'd have a beer or two, they'd drive home. Perhaps they'd even do what they hadn't done for a long time, since it was her husband's last night home for a while.

'I'm running them down now.' Tony had appeared suddenly at the door and caught her smiling to herself.

'Saw sense, did you?' she said. 'Paid her off, did you?' He lifted the truck keys from the labelled hook by the door.

'The girl changed her mind, Dolores. You know what

117

I'm saying? She was a good worker, a real good worker. And now I gotta find me another deck-hand for tomorrow. Expect me when you see me.'

'What about supper?'

'What about it!' He let the door slam at his back.

The girl climbed in last. Dolores watched as the truck turned in the drive. She continued watching as the vehicle disappeared and re-appeared again as it passed the Laceys' lilac tree. She knew every turn in that road, knew the landscape as far as she could see it. That was all she'd ever asked for. Not Margie. Margie couldn't wait to get away. Even the last time she came home. Picked her up at a gas station miles down the highway. Three in the morning and five below. Huddled in the phone booth, blue with cold. Icicles in her hair. Why didn't you call? Dolores had said, Your father would have sent you the fare. Margie had given no explanations. Of course the girl was upset, but so were her parents. And how could they help if she didn't tell them anything? Of course they were mad at her for hitching a ride: it was dangerous, even round their way.

The sun was setting on the water when the truck pulled up on the wharf. The girl jumped down, slung her kit on her back, waved and turned away. From Dolores's window, she looked small, out there on the empty cobbles, weaving through the long shadows cast by the packing sheds.

Margie hadn't even waited until morning before she was up and away again, without a word. You don't know your own mind, Dolores had said, fussing round her with cocoa and towels. You gotta know your own mind. You gotta face up to things as they are. Your trouble is, you've no staying power. Who needs it? Margie'd replied, and laughed like her own mother was crazy.

The girl had reached the highway and Dolores, in spite of herself, could not help transforming the solitary figure into that of her daughter. She could not help worrying.

THE FACTS OF LIFE

Dear Brigitta,

Here's a new rhyme. You can teach it to your pals. You make a big circle and somebody has to stand in the middle and do the actions.

> She's got legs like Betty Grable
> She's got a figure like Marilyn Monroe
> She's got hair like Ginger Rogers
> And a face like an elephant's toe   SO
> Salome, Salome, you should see Salome
> Hands in air, skirts in air, you should see Salome.

Are you missing us? We're missing you. Everybody cried for ages when you left but I think some of them were putting it on a bit even if they were sad. Some people think if they make a big fuss it means they care more but it's what you feel inside that counts, isn't it? Some people, like Sadie Watts, can turn on the waterworks any time they want. When Crooky told Sadie she's got another think coming if she imagines she can get away with insolent behaviour in *her* class, Sadie squeezed out as many tears as if she'd been watching Gone With The Wind. When Crooky turned back to the blackboard, Sadie laughed her head off. School's stupid. If it wasn't for playtime and dinnertime it would be bloody hell. I bet school's better in Sweden. I bet it's better anywhere in the whole world.

Must go. I've got a hundred lines to do for tomorrow. I MUST NOT SNIGGER. In my best writing.

Love from Jennifer.

She licks the envelope, slips the folded letter inside, sticks it down. She places it on her dressing-table then lifts up the lid of her jewellery box. It begins to play the theme tune to the film of Romeo and Juliet *and the ballet-dancer in the pink plastic tutu spins on a lake of blue glass. She takes out a necklace, a string of lilac imitation pearls, with a gilt clip. She fastens it around her neck and looks at herself in the mirror. She sees an ordinary girl of nearly twelve with hair that is not fair enough to be called blonde, not dark enough to be called brown. She's always wanted to be a blonde, like Brigitta, who had silky hair that hung like a bell around her shoulders. If she turns off the lamp and sits directly by the open curtain, the streetlight picks out the highlights in her hair so that it appears to be real natural blonde. She opens two buttons of her nightdress so that the necklace glows against her throat.*

Dear Brigitta,

You mean you've got every afternoon off school? No school dinners at all? Brilliant. I wish I was Swedish. Do you still remember everybody over here now you're back with your old pals? I've got to tell you. Remember Pearl Doig? She's really done it. More than just the once too, so Sadie says. And – in the shelter! Which is our den. She'd no right going with a boy there. It's girls only and anyway she's not even in the gang. We didn't know until it was too late because she dogged off gym with Jimmy Mackeson. Out the main gate and into Baccy Mackie's for three Senior Service and Wrigley's Spearmint to take the smell off her breath. Up the graveyard and along the lane by the burn. Pearl's got a bust, that's what it is. See, if you get past the lovebite and on to a feel (at the top) and you havny any bust, there's nothing for a boy to feel, is there? It's got to be right down to the skin to count, not just over the clothes. So there's no point in stuffing a bra with your mum's old nylons, like some people. I'm dying for a bra but my mum says she's not spending good money on something there's no call for. I must I must increase my bust. Even if you're wee and dumpy like Pearl, a bust makes you look grown up. I wish I had just enough to fill a Teen Line A Cup. Have you got anything at the top?

Love Jennifer.

She opens the top drawer of the dressing-table. She extracts a lipstick from a pile of vests and knickers. She paints a pearly white mouth over the real pink one. She tries out a few poses with the slippery white lips. If her teeth show they look yellow by comparison, so she doesn't smile. She sucks in her cheeks as she's seen Sadie do, and pouts. She lowers her eyes and lets her hair fall over her face. She still doesn't quite look like the kind of girl Elvis couldn't resist.

My dear Brigi,

Today we had a measuring session at the den. Sadie couldn't bring her tape measure because her mum was making her a pop art trouser suit for the summer dance and was working on it morn noon and night to get it finished in time. I had to sneak out my Gran's tape measure from the mending basket. I couldn't tell her what it was for because she'd have said Pride Goes Before a Fall and I'd have got a red face which is worse than anything. Except being sick. I hate hate hate being sick. I'd rather die but d'you know what? Sadie actually makes herself spew. At Izzy's birthday party she stuffed herself stupid and then stuck her fingers down her throat so she wouldn't get fat from all the fairy cakes she ate. Sadie's off her head. Pearl Doig's a fallen woman.

With love from Jenny.

p.s. I'm only a 27 which is just pathetic.
p.p.s. Do you know what Bastard means?

She addresses the sealed envelope, adding the word PRIVATE *to back and front. She puts her envelope in her school-bag beside her pencil case and jotter, copiously decorated with the phrases* Elvis is Fab *and* I love Elvis. *She kicks off her slippers and throws herself on the bed. She stares at the wallpaper. Old-fashioned ballerinas wearing long dresses and garlands in their hair are posed pensively at regular intervals on the pink background. It was what kids had. She wanted purple walls and posters now. Would she get to change it? The wallpaper was still quite new and clean. Would she have to wait for years and years to paint it over?*

My Dear Friend Brigi,

I've found out about that word. If Pearl Doig's really done it – and she told Sadie she's got proof – she could be up the pole with a bastard. And then she'd be sick all the time. She'd want coal and raw fish for her tea every night and that would be the end of her. She'd have to go to a home somewhere in the middle of nowhere and nobody would ever see her again. Not until years later when she'd come back as an old woman with the bastard all grown up and it would look like Pearl and Jimmy Mackeson all mixed together. If it was a girl it would be wee and dumpy with a big bust. But it would have red hair like Jimmy too. And freckles and yellow cats' eyes, yuck! And if it was a boy it would be the same without the freckles. And pink cheeks in place of them. And frizzy hair like a pot-scourer and a gap between his teeth. Nobody speaks to Pearl any more, except Jimmy Mackeson.

From your bosom friend Jenny.

p.s. What did you mean about not wanting to wear a bra even when your bust grows? You've definitely got to wear one then or it will all fall down. You'll not be able to run about without everybody watching it bouncing. No bras and no stockings? And lipstick's bad for you? I don't know if I'd like Sweden after all.

She stands at the open window listening to the screech of bicycle wheels skidding down the hill at the end of the street, and the bursts of laughter from those who haven't yet been called home, the big boys with ice-blue jeans and black reefer jackets who totally ignore kids like her.

Dear B,

Hello again. That was quick and thanks for putting on so many stamps. I'm hoping to swap them with my brother – who's a mean pig – for his Story of Pop cards, specially this fab one he's got of Elvis. Do you like Elvis or Cliff? I just love Elvis. I'll always just love Elvis. Every time I see a photo of him I go all shivery inside. Do you ever get that feeling, you know the one I mean, like when you go on the Rib Tickler at the shows and you think your belly's spinning round inside you. Pearl told Sadie – when Sadie was still talking to her – that you get that feeling if you go all the way. I don't see how an ordinary boy could make you feel like that, whatever he did.

I must get dressed now. It's Sadie's birthday and we're all going to The Rio to see James Bond in From Russia With Love. Sadie had to promise her mum not to make herself sick after the choc-ices and popcorn. If she doesn't stop making herself sick on purpose she's getting sent to a headshrinker.

Yours truly, J.

p.s. Sadie and Izzy said to say hello and what are the Swedish boys like? Do they all have blonde hair? What are they like at kissing and how far do you go?

She puts on her favourite skirt, a purple one, and a matching polo-neck jersey. She turns to look at herself sideways in the mirror. She takes a deep breath and holds her tummy in until it is as flat as possible. She walks stiffly downstairs, maintaining this uncomfortable, if flattering position.

Dear B,

You mean you actually saw him with nothing on, not a stitch and it wasn't even dark? And your mum knew about it? My mum would have a fit at the very idea. I'd never ever tell her about anything like that. The other day we were playing strip jack naked, me and Izzy and Gegs and Tommy Swan who thinks he's god's gift just because he got to go to Spain on his holidays and he's still got the tan. Tommy Swan wanted to lose, you could tell. He had a dirty big grin on his face when he got down to his Y's but I bet he'd have crapped out in the end even if his mum hadn't bawled his name across the estate and he'd had to go home for his tea that instant. I was quite glad we had to stop really. I wouldn't have known where to look if he'd taken everything off.

Sweden must be a funny place. Do people take off their clothes in front of other people just like that? I don't think even Pearl and Jimmy took everything off when they did it in the den. I don't think they even did it lying down because the floor's so manky you'd have to be off your head to lie down on it.

I never really told you about the den. It's creepy and a bit smelly but it's fab. There's yellow ivy all over it and you'd never know it was there if you didn't go right up close. The ivy's camouflage. The army must have grown it long ago so the Germans couldn't see that it was an air-raid shelter. And bomb it. There's not been a war here for centuries, well anyway it's twenty-five years since the Battle of Britain, I know that because my brother's been spending all his pocket money on Battle of Britain stamps. He swapped me a photo of Elvis – at last! – for all the Swedish stamps I saved from your letters. Now I've got Elvis under my pillow and I can look at him any time I want. Fab. Thanks again for the stamps.

Hoping to hear from you soon. Yours, Jen.

She puts the letter in the usual hiding place and climbs into bed. From under her pillow she brings out her cherished photo of Elvis, smiling like an advertisement for toothpaste, his dark hair slicked back, his glittering eyes gazing straight at her. She kisses it passionately, slips it back into her pillowcase and switches off the light.

Dear B,

It was a den day today. I got there first and I had no matches to light my candle so I had to wait for Sadie. If you don't have a candle lit, the den's as black as the devil's armpit. Armpits are yuck, aren't they? Do you have hair in yours yet? I don't want any ever ever ever. But Sadie says you can't stop it coming. It's evolution which is part of growing up. And so is sweating. I hate sweating. Wet spots on your shirt. Smelly wet spots. I hate smells. You can't stop *them* either. And you can't stop you-know-what starting. I don't fancy *that* at all. Pearl Doig can keep it for all I care, even if it goes with having a bust. Sadie says you can't go swimming when it's your time of the month and

I love swimming. I want to be a deep-sea diver when I grow up so I can sit in a glass-bottomed boat and float across a coral reef until I see a giant oyster and I dive off the side in my black wet-look swimsuit and silver flippers and fight an octopus before I get to the oyster, but I get to it just before my oxygen runs out and then I swim to the surface where my boyfriend – who looks like Elvis and The Saint and James Bond – but younger – all rolled into one – is waiting for me to come up with the treasure. And he sweeps me into his arms because he's madly in love with me.

Your very own friend in Scotland, J.xx

Dear Brigitta,

Today was Practising. That's what everybody really comes to the den for. Sadie chooses partners and we take turns. I got paired off with Izzy. Everybody else watches while you practise and gives you marks out of ten. Izzy says I kiss better than Tommy Swan who she nearly got off with when she was down the scout hut. She says his lips were too hard and she came out in a rash. Anyway, me and Izzy were kissing and everybody else was watching. Sadie couldn't have barred the door properly today because in comes, who do you think? Pearl Doig and Jimmy Mackeson! Sadie told them to get lost, it was our den and no boys were allowed and Pearl says, Who says? And everybody says, We do. Jimmy's saying nothing, just standing there, lighting up a fag and smirking. And what's so great about you lot, then? says Pearl. Look who's talking, says Sadie, everybody knows what *she* is. Salome, Salome, you should see Salome, Sadie chants and we all begin clapping. Hands in air, skirts in air, You should see Salome. Ha, ha, ha, says Pearl, shaking her shoulders so her bust jiggles and putting her arms round wee Jimmy. Ha, ha, ha, you think I'm bad? You don't know anything, she says. You don't even know the facts of life. I'm a woman, a real woman. You lot, she says, you know what you lot are? Perverts, she says. Bloody perverts.

I don't think I'm going back to the den. I really want to be a real woman very soon. But not quite yet.

J.XXX

SNAKES AND LADDERS

LILY PICKED AT THE HEM OF her coatsleeve while she waited. She was wearing her good coat today – at least, it used to be good but now it was fraying at the cuffs. Since Sammy went into hospital she had been losing weight and her clothes, as well as being shabby, drooped over her narrow shoulders. It didn't seem worth cooking a proper dinner just for one, and besides, skipping meals saved money. Not that there was ever any to save.

The waiting room smelled of disinfectant, like the hospital. The doctors there told her, when she could get hold of one, that Sammy was making some improvement but she didn't notice any. The therapist said that he was interested in clay and had him throwing fistfuls of it at the wall. Something about frustration, the therapist said, but there was more to it than that. Everyone in her area must be frustrated if frustration meant throwing things. There were broken windows all over. Sammy would be normal if that was all there was to it. They were giving him drugs to regulate his behaviour – that's what they said – but the drugs just made him talk a lot of nonsense or loll around with his mouth hanging open. He was like a lump of clay himself on those sedatives. He still screamed if anyone mentioned a cupboard. One day he threw himself at the wall.

'Number eight, please.' A thin woman got up, tugging at the man next to her. He grunted, heaved to his feet and slouched after her through the door marked INTERVIEWS. The door clicked shut. Lily's plastic card had a nine on it so she would be next. She bit a ragnail and fixed her eyes on a poster directly opposite her. There was nothing else to look at. In large black letters it commanded:

TAKE PRIDE IN YOUR ENVIRONMENT
DON'T SPOIL IT WITH LITTER

The words were printed on a stretch of very green grass, sprinkled with daisies. Right in the middle of the meadow lay a pile of crisp packets and broken beer bottles. Who'd want to spoil such lovely grass? Lily couldn't remember seeing grass which looked as green. There was nothing in the poster which looked at all like Lily's area except the litter though even that looked wrong. You could sweep *that* up in a minute. Litter, as Lily knew it, meant streets of rotting filth which spewed out of drains every time it rained and crawled further and further up the walls of the flats. And the grass wasn't green, like that. It was nearer the colour of dishwater.

'Number nine, please.' The number eight people slammed the waiting-room door behind them as they left. Lily went into the interview-room, holding out her number. The young clerk coughed briskly into his fist. He scraped his chair forward until he was tucked in tightly behind his desk. He began thumbing through a pile of forms.

Lily smiled, noting that his shirt was missing a button. Needs looking after, she thought, just like Sammy.

'Now then. Your name is Marsh, Lily Marsh, is that correct?' The clerk spread his arms across the polished wood and leaned towards Lily. She nodded in reply.

'And you're divorced, Mrs Marsh, am I right? And reside at 125 Hill View, 14/B, Easter Drumbeath?

'Yes.'

'And I understand you've applied for a transfer?'

'That's right. I want to move to another area.'

The clerk pulled a green form from the pile. It was a dull colour, a bit like the doors on the flats at her end of Hill View, where you couldn't see the hills. You could see the quarry though, a great lake of yellow mud. The council had re-painted the doors on the other end of the street a year past, but they'd stopped half-way.

'You see, my son's no well. He's in the hospital. He had a terrible shock . . .' At that moment the clerk was overwhelmed by a fit of sneezing. 'You should be in your bed,' said Lily. The young man coughed then gave her a bleary smile.

'Yes I . . . no I'm afraid . . . some of us must keep going,' he replied, as though remembering a motto. He straightened up his papers.

'Now, can we go through this step by step, if you please.' He glanced at the clock while he spoke. 'You say your son resides with you?'

'He stays with me, yes. But we cannae go on staying where we are.'

The clerk sighed, stubbed his pencil against the desk, took a deep breath. 'I'm aware that Easter Drumbeath is not the most desirable housing area but there's a long list for houses anywhere. Easter Drumbeath houses forty thousand tenants and I would say, at a modest estimate, twenty per cent of them have applied for a transfer within the last five years. Do you know how many people that is, Mrs Marsh? Thousands!

'I know it's hard for other people in Drum. The place is in a terrible state. It's like . . .' her fingers twisted into her cuffs, 'like the inside of a litter bin.'

'Ah, but you see, the council cannot be held responsible for litter. After all, who drops the litter?'

'It's not just that,' Lily began but the clerk still had his eye on the clock.

'I must explain to you that the council allocates rehousing through what we call a point system.' He raised his eyes to the ceiling, as though he were trying to remember his lines. 'This is based on the present condition of the tenant's housing. I must emphasise that the waiting-list is extremely long and, in all fairness, would be better closed for the time being. Even if your points do add up to the required number, it is likely to be a considerable time before the relocation takes place. With the situation as it is, it might be better not to raise people's hopes. Do you see what I mean, Mrs Marsh?'

The clerk peered at Lily with such weary eyes that she felt obliged to nod, although she wanted to ask about the point system and relocation and how long a 'considerable time' was likely to be. But she didn't want to be a nuisance.

'Let's start with you, Mrs Marsh. Do you work?'

'No.'

'What about your ex-husband? Does he provide any

maintenance?' Lily answered the first string of questions to the top of the clerk's head while he ticked off boxes on the green form.

'I have a note here to the effect that you are behind with your rent payments.'

'It's only three weeks behind,' she replied. 'It's the first time. You see, my son's in the hospital and the new payment scheme's not working properly yet.'

'There was a circular, Mrs Marsh, supplying advance information relating to the delay. You were advised to make alternative arrangements.'

Lily had received the letter but couldn't make alternative arrangements. She couldn't borrow money. Who was there to borrow from? No one she knew had money to spare and the pawn wouldn't give her anything for her belongings. The bus fares to the hospital, they added up.

'Still,' said the clerk, 'I imagine many people in Easter Drumbeath are in the same position. We'll try to find out what can be said in your favour, shall we? For instance, if you are lacking in some basic amenity, like a clean water-supply, or electricity, it will be easier to push a transfer through.'

'They're going to cut off my electricity soon. I can't pay the bill.' Lily hadn't intended to mention the electric but the clerk seemed to be saying that having it cut off would help.

'I'm afraid that's no good, Mrs Marsh. If it had already been cut off, it might have made a difference but we can only take the present situation into consideration.'

'But the flats are damp,' said Lily. 'I've got to keep the fire on all the time. There's damp all over the walls, in big black patches.' The clerk took a note of this. The word 'damp' was given a tick. One point to Lily. It was as if the pair of them were playing a strange game of snakes and ladders, with Lily landing on more than her fair share of snakes. When the clerk reached the bottom of the third page of questions, there remained a small space without any boxes.

'Now, are there any particular circumstances you'd like to mention in the "Comments" section?' Lily had been trying to tell the clerk about Sammy right from the start and now there was just this little space left without any boxes.

'He had a breakdown, my son Sammy. He had a terrible shock and then he had a breakdown.' She paused. Would there be room for any more?

'Go on, Mrs Marsh.'

'There was this empty flat . . . on the floor below. Sammy used to go in there sometimes to . . . just to look around, for something to do . . .' She couldn't say that he brought her floorboards for firewood. 'He was poking around, just looking at things. He'd told me about a funny smell coming from a cupboard. I said it would be the damp because everything smells rotten when it's damp. The cupboard was locked. I said he shouldn't force it, I told him to leave well alone. But you know what kids are like. He got the door open. And there he was!'

'Who was, Mrs Marsh?'

'Mr Martin, from flat eleven, hanging from a rope, poor man. There were . . . things moving all over him. Poor Sammy. Poor Mr Martin. Sorry!' Lily choked to a halt.

The young man was embarrassed by the weeping

woman in front of him but he had come across this kind of thing before. Sometimes it was just a try-on.

'So this ah . . . this breakdown you say your son had, this would have occurred as a result . . . of the shock of seeing this ah . . . corpse?' Lily lowered her head. 'I do sympathise with you, Mrs Marsh. I'll try to do what I . . .' The clerk's condolences were cut short by another irrepressible sneeze.

Lily walked home along the canal. It was a long walk but it helped to pass the time. It was a bright day and the sun stroked the back of her neck like a warm fingertip. Towards the end of the landscaped walkway, she began to start noticing the litter. A piece of broken bottle had trapped the sun on its curve and shone fiercely. A wisp of smoke curled round the jagged edge. Below the glass, the weeds were scorched.

She climbed through the torn fence where Easter Drumbeath's tangle of cement walkways snaked across the motorway. This was where the gardens abruptly came to an end, where the bird-song petered out. In Drumbeath the birds didn't stay long, except for the scavenging gulls: and they didn't sing, they squawked.

She glanced back at the neat bungalows and their well-tended lawns. She'd always wanted a garden, a small one would do fine, a lawn set off with a blaze of colour in the flower-beds. But they'd never give her a garden. On the path, the broken bottle had started a small fire. How easy that would be, she thought. She had heard of folk who'd done such things.

When she arrived at the centre, she counted out her

change and stopped at one of the few shops which wasn't an off-licence or a betting shop. A row of fortresses, grilled and barred with iron. No one wanted a shop here anymore. The insurance was too high, the break-ins too frequent, even with the iron bars and electronic alarms. She pushed open the heavy door.

The man behind the counter was filling in a pools coupon and smoking between coughs. On the counter lay a pile of shrivelled oranges next to slabs of sausage-meat and discoloured bacon. The radio crackled out a song about the bright city lights of somewhere else.

'Yeah?' said the shopkeeper, without looking up.

'How much is a gallon of paraffin?' Lily asked, as casually as possible.

REPEAT PLEASE

SHE RINGS THE DOORBELL. SHE SPEAKS through the entryphone. It is noon. She is always on time, sometimes a little bit early. She says *Hello it's Jane. Teacher.* Teacher Jane thinks I do not remember her voice from one week to the next. I press the button and the downstairs door opens for her. I wait for her to knock on my door.

When Teacher Jane knocks on my door I open it. This is the arrangement. She comes once a week to teach me English words. She says *Hello how are you.* She smiles a big smile. She wants that I say *I am very well thank you.* I say only *Come* and she follows me inside.

I am not so very well thank you. I am cold. Since I have been here, since I came down the steps of the plane at London three years ago I feel as if the sun has not touched me. It rained the day I arrived, not the rain we have at home, not the big bright drops which crash down and vanish. Here the rain wraps itself around you like a wet sari.

Ali met me at the airport. He was holding an umbrella and a raincoat. He gave me the coat. He told me I would need a coat. He took my suitcase and began walking. I followed

138

him. We travelled by bus, by train. We walked up a windy street and stopped at the downstairs door. He showed me my name next to his on the entryphone. We walked up the stairs. He took me inside. The flat was empty. He told me this would be home. It is not home. It is only a house.

When Teacher Jane comes I am tired. Since Izmir was born I do not sleep. I try to sleep but the baby wakes me, or my dreams do.

I am walking, feeling the hot earth under my feet. I am walking to the river, the wide slow yellow river. Beside me is my sister. She has her small pitcher on her head. A plane crosses the sky and we look up. It is not one of the great white birds which brings wives to husbands across the world. It is small and black, buzzing. My sister does not know the difference. She waves at it and runs down the bank into the water.

When Jane rings my doorbell I do not want to answer it. I do not want this to be my door. I cannot step outside into the yard and throw rice to the chickens. I cannot pick fruit from the tree. Teacher Jane says *Hello how are you*. I say only *Come* because that is all that is necessary. Jane is not doctor. She is teacher of words only. She cannot make baby eat, cannot mend my dreams. She cannot find Ali a better job. He goes out in the morning, early. He comes home in the middle of the night. I get up, prepare some food. He eats, he tells me how many curries were sold at the restaurant. He smokes some cigarettes and goes to sleep. Ali goes to sleep and I lie beside him, waiting for the baby to wake up.

We wade until we are waist deep. We begin to wash, my sister splashing and ducking her head underwater. On the far bank, the ferry is loading up with passengers, the local ferry which has standing room only, in one straight line. I count seven women, one little old man.

On the far bank it is peaceful. There is a temple, a small tea plantation and a forest of tall trees. My grandfather told us that these trees came all the way from Scotland. He would go to the forest often, to walk, he'd say, but with only one leg he did not walk so much. Mostly he would sleep in the shade of the Scottish trees.

Teacher Jane sits on the bed and opens her bag. She takes out a notebook and a pencil. This is the lesson beginning. She empties the contents of her bag on to the floor, piece by piece. She stops at each item and says its name. She says this name two or three times then I must *Repeat please*. When Jane's bag is empty – and my room is untidy again – she asks me the names again and I remember one or two. Paper, pencil, book – always Jane has books and newspapers and magazines. I think in her house she must have only books and magazines because each time she brings different ones. In my house there is only the Asian newspaper. Ali reads it. I use it to wrap up the vegetable peelings.

After I have said paper, pencil, book, diary, hairbrush, cigarettes, matches, keyring, we do her shopping. She holds up a carrot. *Carrot*, she says. She lays it beside the hairbrush and points to the hairbrush. *Carrot?* she says. She wants me to say, *No, it's not a carrot, it's a hairbrush.* I say only, *No*. This is not important to me. The baby is important, and Ali. I have no room in my heart for carrots and hairbrushes. I will not make this house into a home because I know the English word for a vegetable I do not very much like.

Ali says I must learn to speak English so that he can go on longer trips to his brother's house in Leeds. There is not enough room for all of us to visit. Anyway, Ali is going on business. I do not know what business. Ali says I do not need to know. We do not agree about this and I worry in case he is maybe doing something dangerous. But money must be sent to our home town somehow and in the restaurant he earns so little.

Baby wakes up. *Baby crying*, says Jane. I too say *Baby crying* and Jane says, *Good*. But now she must sit, not teaching, while I feed Izmir. I do not have enough milk. I am a poor cow. When Izmir has emptied each breast he cries for more. I get the tinned milk. They gave it to me at the clinic. I show it to Jane. *OK*? I say. *Sorry*, says Jane. I point to the writing. I want her to read the instructions on the tin. I want her to teach me the right mixture but she doesn't understand. Why does she teach me the words for carrots and hairbrushes and not *Help me please*? All Jane does is stare at Izmir's tiny crumpled face and be afraid. Afraid that just by looking she will make the crying worse. Afraid that if she held him in her arms he would break.

The ferry is standing at the platform. And then the sudden disturbance at the bank, the ferryman running into the forest, the boat sliding away from the bank without its oars, the boat rocking, the monkeys screeching as the black plane returns, low this time, roaring, trailing a filthy ribbon of smoke. And then the rattle of gunfire and the ferry passengers tossed like logs into the water. The river is streaked with red. This is my sleeping dream. It will not go away. It is the past and the past will not go away. My grandfather was dead by the time he was brought ashore, the river mud streaming over his body.

My waking dream is of the future. It also will not go away. Ali tells me I live too much in my imagination and that I will be happier here, will feel safer here once I have learned more about this country, once I learn English. He says I must put everything from home behind me. He says I must spend more time outside, looking around me, and not so much time inside myself. He says when Izmir is older, he can play in front of the house. There is a small concrete yard. I have planted some flowers out there, by the wall, but I do not sit in the yard and Izmir will not play there when he is older. I will not let him. My waking dream will not let me leave him there. In my mind I see a car stopping, a grey car with dark windows. Two men get out. I cannot tell what they look like, only that they are dressed in suits and wear dark glasses. Everything happens in a flash.

When I tell Ali my dream, he asks me if they are Asian men or white men. I do not know but I know there is a reason and it is Izmir they want, not the fair-haired child next door. There is no accident. They pull Izmir off his toy train, bundle him into the car and drive off. Ali says these things happen here only on the television.

The lesson begins again when Izmir has cried himself to sleep. Jane fetches the clock from the windowledge and points to the time. *Half-past twelve*, she says. She makes the hands move round the clock and tells me the time. *One o'clock. What time is it*? and I must *Repeat please*. At one o'clock Jane will pack up her bag and go away. I want her to go because I am tired yet I do not like to be alone, in this house which is not a home.

Jane sees me yawning before she has finished with the time, so she puts back the clock. She smiles and says *Sleepy*? and I say *Sleepy*, then *Tea*? and she says *Thank you very much*. We go into the kitchen, leaving Izmir asleep in his pram. There is now a table and two chairs. While we are drinking our tea I hear a small noise at the door. *Postman*? says Jane. *Postman*, I say. *Letters*, says Jane. I will fetch the letters when Jane goes away.

Jane wants to show me something special. She has a magazine with a shiny cover. She turns the pages. There are pictures of watches and cars and men in English suits and girls in short dresses. Also of perfume bottles and underwear and big country houses. Also of soldiers and operations and mountains. She stops at a photograph of a mountain covered with trees. These are the Scottish trees my grandfather was so fond of. I have been living in this country for three years now. I have not seen any of these trees, except in December little ones which are taken indoors and dressed up.

Look, says Jane. She turns the page and points. It is my own village, my own river. There is no ferryboat at the landing. There are no people laying out laundry on the bank or washing in the river but I know they are all there somewhere, out of sight, watching the pictures being taken, standing maybe right behind the photographer, telling him what to put in his picture. Did my sister too run over and watch or was she still too frightened of that spot?

Your home, says Jane. She is very happy to be showing

me the river, but I cannot see that peaceful empty river. The noise is in my ears, the buzzing and the roars, the rattles and the screams. And the smell of burning fills my nostrils. I close my eyes to block out the bloody picture I see taking shape over the peaceful one and I am thinking, yes, Ali is right: I live too much in my imagination, and then Jane is jumping up from the table and shaking my arm and shouting *Look! Look!*, and I see smoke creeping round the door and I know that the smell of burning is not a phantom from the past but is the present, is here, now, in my house. Jane stands back as I run for Izmir.

The hall is black with smoke. At the door is a burning ball of rags and the carpet and the wallpaper have caught fire and I know now that it was not the postman who came today. I am filling up buckets of water at the sink and Jane is throwing the water at the fire in between shouting through the open window, *Fire! Fire!*, and *Help! Help!*, and I am repeating again and again everything she says as loudly and clearly as I can.

THE NEW CAFÉ

'CUP OF TEA, PLEASE.'

Alice ignored the request. There were times when the walls of her small but popular café seemed to close in on her, times like this, when all the prep for lunch should have been finished but wasn't, when a customer was waiting to be served and Ben, her stage-struck assistant, had left the counter unattended.

'Excuse me . . .'

At times like this, who needed interruptions? Adding the final touches to a dish – putting its face on, Ben called it – was the only part of the daily routine which Alice still enjoyed when she found time to spend on it, but was there ever a spare moment?

With one hand she ladled wine over the trout; with the other, she rapidly stirred a sauce.

'Cup of tea, please,' the flat, insistent voice repeated.

At times like this, Alice felt like tossing her apron in the air and walking out. What had begun five years ago as a bid for independence, an alternative to redundancy, had turned into a treadmill. One which was always turning too fast.

'Someone will be with you. Shortly.'

'I asked already. I waited already.'

Alice spun round to confront the customer, arms folded, proprietorial, but drew back at the sight of the woman facing her: she was too ragged for it to be an affectation. Her coat was a filthy unseasonal fur, bald in patches; her dress a threadbare evening garment on which the counter lights showed up every stain and tear. Alice didn't want to serve her. Not this kind of customer. Not now, just before the lunch rush. She resolved, as Ben had often suggested, to upgrade the *Soup Kitchen* from counter to table service.

'We don't sell *cups* of tea. Only pots . . . It's quite expensive that way.'

The woman didn't take the hint. She dug into a ripped pocket, pulled out a handful of change and lined it up on the counter with a cracked, black fingernail. 'Is that enough for a pot, then?'

Alice wanted to say, It's nothing personal, we just need all the tables for diners, but it was the late-morning lull, the dining-room was empty, so what could she say? She busied herself with the sauce on the stove.

'Am I to get my tea or not?' The woman's loose lips widened into a squint grin, as if she had read Alice's thoughts, and were issuing a challenge. And her pale eyes – weren't they somehow familiar? – roamed the café boldly as if she of all people were making an assessment.

The radio hammered out its midday jingle, a reminder to Alice that if the food didn't go into the oven immediately, it wouldn't be ready for lunch. She swept up the change and slapped teapot, milk jug, cup, saucer and spoon on to the woman's tray. Ben was right. A minimum charge over lunchtime was what was needed.

As if on cue, Ben appeared when Mrs Bills, who had the shop across the road, flounced through the doorway, trailing an odour of perfumed mothball. A jeweller's widow, she was one of the regulars, most of whom were antique or bric-à-brac dealers with shops in the neighbourhood of the Lane.

The area attracted its own particular crowd; small-time crooks, who gossiped and eavesdropped in doorways, finicky collectors who tapped and poked in the dusty cluttered stores and a mixed bag of local dealers. It was a predatory environment. Deception was a way of life and a torn jersey rarely signified that its owner was out at the elbow. Mrs Bills, for instance, dressed like a tinker down to her cuffs, below which twinkled gems as big as her knuckles.

Alice washed out the breakfast cups while Ben lounged at the counter, catching up on the street gossip. Her assistant was good with the regulars and, to a stranger, it might seem as though the café were his and Alice, who seldom took time off to chat, were the hired help.

The woman in the dirty fur scuffed off the premises just as Mrs Bills left the counter.

'What a state!' Ben declared, closing the door firmly at the woman's back. 'I wouldn't have served *her*. And I'd have been doing you a favour. People like that are bad for business.' He flicked crumbs from the counter with a corner of his dishtowel. 'You know,' he continued, 'she reminds me of this character. Mother Courage. A racketeer if ever there was one. We've been rehearsing Brecht for

147

ages. So dismal.' Ben usually managed to bring drama into his conversation. The *Soup Kitchen* was his bread and butter, the stage his rarely tasted jam.

The woman returned a few days later, this time on a wet, dreary afternoon.

'*Pot* of tea for one, please.'

Soaked, she looked even worse than before, hair plastered against her collar, eye make-up dribbling into the deep scores etched on her face. Same coat, same dress. But also a battered black hat sewn round with cloth poppies, a hat which – how long? fifteen, no, it must have been twenty years ago – had been Alice's own. With growing dismay, Alice began to recognise, through years of wear and tear, the face of Chrissie Potts beneath her own old hat. Alice called for Ben. 'Take care of the counter, please. We have a customer.'

She turned away, to avoid looking, to think, to compose herself. Twenty years. Could this be the same Chrissie with whom she'd shared bottles of cheap wine in the Glen Hotel where they'd been hired as chambermaids? Hired for the summer. For Alice a stopgap between school and college in the city. For Chrissie the first real job. Alice chopped onions with more than necessary enthusiasm, face firmly averted from the counter. She could hear Ben whistling his disapproval as he dealt out the tea things. He made an intimidating show of his efficiency.

'I see Mother Courage has got herself a hat,' said Ben, when they were alone again. Alice wanted to tell him about her old friend, but what was there to tell? They'd lost touch soon after that short summer. Alice had made new friends at college, and Chrissie? There had been a local man whom she'd been keen on. Had she married him? It was all so long ago. All Alice remembered was Chrissie's optimism. Nothing dissuaded that girl from believing that the best things in life were just round the corner.

'The outfit's perfect for the part . . .'

'D'you mind making a start on tomorrow's soup?'

'Of course,' Ben replied, smirking. 'Mustn't forget the *soup*. What's it to be, Dossers' Broth?'

The pram was becoming a familiar sight in the doorway, as was Chrissie at the café's best table, where she spent hours staring at her image in the wall mirror. Why, Alice asked herself repeatedly, had she not acknowledged Chrissie when she first recognised her? At least given her a late lunch, sat down for a chat. But when did she ever sit down? And now the right moment had passed. Besides, what would there be to say after all this time?

In spite of complaints about Chrissie's unsociable odour – complaints which Ben reported back with relish – Alice did nothing more than open the windows wide. She had become used and somehow looked forward to Chrissie's visits, though she made a point of having Ben serve her. And she had recently noticed a drop in the takings as well as the absence of some of the regulars.

'Why don't you concentrate a bit more on your paying customers,' said Ben. 'Unless it's a *real* soup kitchen you want.'

Alice stuffed the empty gin bottle deep into the bin. With undisguised contempt Ben had informed her that Chrissie had fallen into a stupor, her face pressed against the mirror. Until now, there had been no evidence of Chrissie drinking on the premises.

'You'll never get your wine licence this way,' said Ben. 'And, by the way, did you know that there's a new place opening round the corner. Upmarket. Speaking to the manager the other day. Mentioned that he was looking for help. Wants somebody who knows the area . . .'

Since Chrissie's visits had become regular, Ben had been threatening to look for another job, somewhere in which the right people congregated, where people like Chrissie didn't get over the doorstep. Alice couldn't afford to lose him, not now, with the summer season approaching. There was no time to train a replacement, no time even to look for one.

'Okay,' said Alice. 'I'll tell her she's got to go.'

'About time,' said Ben. 'But maybe I should do it for you. Give the situation a bit of drama. I do a good authority figure.'

'No,' said Alice. 'I'll tell her . . .'

Chrissie, noticeably drunk, was tottering towards the counter, coat flapping, hat in hand. Ben slowly polished a dinner plate, and glared. Chrissie leaned over the counter, placed the battered hat firmly on Alice's head, then turned and reeled into the street.

'Take it off!' Ben screeched. 'It's probably infested!'

Alice reached up to her head as if she were dazed. She removed the hat and began turning it round in her hands. The cloth poppies flopped against the limp brim. Ben stood back, watching the hat as if it were alive.

'Mind you,' Ben said at length, 'it must have been a good hat once. Maybe I could have it fumigated. The one we've got in Costumes isn't as lived-in as that.'

'It stays here,' Alice insisted, 'in case she comes back.'

It was a fine day, the first good day for weeks. The bright sunlight poked through streaks of grime on the windows. Spring cleaning. Something else Alice would have to find time for. She felt as though her life were being eaten up by the endless cycle of café chores – the shopping, preparation, cooking, serving, clearing up, the shopping, preparation and so it went on. She could hear the pram-wheels creak as a hatless Chrissie passed the antique jewellery shop, the lamp shop, the old-lace shop. Head bared to the sun, in no hurry to go anywhere, Alice's old friend quit the Lane, laughing all the way to the corner, where the new café was almost ready to open.

A BIT OF BODY

When asked, she looked directly into the mirror at the face above her own, the young, pretty face framed by a sleek black bob, and replied:

I want something different, not too different though, in fact something which has been there all along, just waiting for the right opportunity to reveal itself. It could be ever so slight but it must make a change. I can't go on looking in the mirror and thinking, Who is this? This is the result of circumstances beyond my control, this isn't the real me. Peering out from this tousle of mousy hair, squinting through a straggly fringe, this is a poor approximation of the real Scarlet Smith.

I want something which will make me feel fresh, new. Not that I expect to turn into a different person, no, I've never believed you can evade your personal blueprint. And I can live tolerably well with what I've inherited – the nose that's too big, the eyes which are not quite aligned. Have you noticed the way my left eyebrow strays away from the eye, as if I'm permanently surprised?

Life doesn't surprise me enough. I want to be surprised.

I want to be able to look into the mirror when you've finished and you've done something about the grey and the split ends and the way my hair hangs in limp hanks, like wet wool. I want to be able to look in the mirror and say, Yes, that's right.

When I was your age it was easy. I just washed my hair twice a week and brushed until it shone, fixed it in a clasp or a bow, when bows were the thing. I could go out on the street and people noticed. It was bright, my hair, the kind of colour you don't get from a bottle. It had a glow to it, it had fire.

I want to go out on the street and be noticed. I don't mean I want to turn heads exactly, I mean I don't expect to be treated like a celebrity. I wouldn't have chosen Stewart if that's what I'd been after. I'd have gone for one of the others. There were others, though I'm talking of way back. I don't really want to be noticed as *standing out*. No, nothing ostentatious. Just to feel I belong, that I'm contributing – even if it's just a splash of colour, it's not too much to ask, is it?

Nothing drastic, you understand. Anything too way out would be wrong for me, and I'm sure Stewart would find a big change embarrassing, unnerving and I'd have to wear a hat if we went out together. Not that we're in the habit of that.

Full perm, half perm, highlights, full head colour, rinse and tint, root treatment, split-end singeing. And that's before you people get out your scissors! Trim: from master cutter or straight from the salon floor. I don't know where to start.

I'm really after something which changes more than

153

just my hair, which goes deeper than my appearance, something which will make Stewart sit up and take notice, but subtle so he won't know exactly what's different. Something to make him look twice. And think to himself, Scarlet is looking good. Something natural enough for him to think he'd just not noticed this fact for a while.

Which is quite true. He hasn't noticed me at all and I haven't noticed him. And neither of us are any the worse for it. We get along fine if we don't communicate any more than necessary. Communicating with Stewart is something no one has done successfully for some time. There are reasons for this and I'm familiar with all the medical terminology and have a rough idea what's supposed to be wrong with him. But giving it a name makes it no easier to live with. Conversation with Stewart is in itself a minefield. Too many no-go areas. Too many taboo topics.

And it's quite likely all he'll do is complain about the cost of this outing, even though I only visit a hairdresser's once a year on average and usually it's for a straightforward chop. It's probably not in my interests for Stewart to know I've been here at all. But then, when does he lift his head high enough to notice my hair?

I just catch sight of myself now and again and what do I see? It's someone I don't know looking back at me, someone I didn't intend to become. A wash-out. I don't expect miracles and you're only dealing with my hair – there's nothing you can do about the crow's-feet around the eyes and the creases in the cheeks. But if you could just give my hair a lift – a bit of body, it might restore me to the world. Did you know that when people stop noticing you, you disappear?

The young face above Scarlet Smith is chewing gum and staring into the reflected near distance where a kettle is coming to the boil and two other assistants are gossiping at the service desk. A young man makes faces at them through the window.

The girl's perfectly styled hair shimmers as she picks up a stylebook. She hands it to Scarlet, wraps her in an outsize plastic bib and leaves her to make up her mind.

TESTING, TESTING

CHARLIE SLOMAN INSTALLED HIMSELF IN A forward-facing window seat. He hoped that the train would be quiet. But not deserted. A bit of conversation on the way up wouldn't go wrong. See him through the black spots on the scenery. Take his mind off his condition. A bad heart was something that didn't go away. Irreparable damage, the doctor said. It stays with you. The cross you have to bear.

A bloke sat down opposite. A nondescript face, the kind of features you'd be hard pressed to describe if you had to, for instance on the occasion of an accident or an incident or whatever. The eyebrows just. You might remember the eyebrows, being thick and black and bristly, like iron filings. Otherwise the face matched the weather, colourless.

Compared to his drab companion, Sloman felt he cut something of a dash. His new jersey, saved since last autumn's sales for the Hebridean trip, was a departure from his usual seaman's navy or fisherman's off-white. A golfer's V-neck, flame red, had been his choice. On the left breast, near the heart, a small blue lion stood on its hind legs.

The bloke pulled a rolled-up magazine from his pocket. *Weekend*, Sloman read upside down, *Easter Special*. It had slipped his mind that he'd booked his journey for bang on Good Friday. Easter had never been anything special until he'd begun the annual trips to the island. Now, the holiday had become something of a pilgrimage – nothing religious about it though and any time after the clocks changed would do fine. It was the long evenings he was after, a change of air and the view west at sunset.

He leaned into the aisle and surveyed the carriage. Double seat each. Just right except for that couple with the baby. Parked themselves directly across the way and from the word go a palaver. Toys, bottles and the rest rolling off the table, the wee one whingeing, him with his big crackly newspaper, her with pokes of crisps and sweeties. Sloman could have done without them.

He concentrated on the view as the train clattered along by the Clyde coast. Nothing to please the eye at first but it improved. Once the train began climbing up by the Gareloch there were less of the scrap-yards, more open space, more real scenery – trees, hills, water, that kind of thing. And some of it quite impressive, like that high dark peak arching over the loch like a gigantic jawbone. But still there were blots on the landscape. In the foreground the Ministry of Defence had the monopoly. The open space was sealed off behind jaggy fences and KEEP OUT signs. What did go on, Sloman wondered, beneath the surface of that lead-grey water?

– Doesny bear thinking about, he said.

The bloke opposite nodded. He slid a finger into his

magazine and flipped over to the centrefold. Sloman saw an upside-down dolly bird in a red corset, black fishnet gloves and legwear. He averted his eyes. There might be a time and place for it but this wasn't the time. Not Easter. A bit respect was called for. Not that he'd ever been one for religion but you couldn't deny it all outright, could you? You couldn't be sure some of that stuff in the bible wasn't true. Anyway, the point was not that a dead body came back to life, that had to be open to question. But leaving that aside, the fact remained that three men on a certain day, met their deaths nailed to wooden crosses on a hill. That kind of thing was well-documented fact. It was common practice in the bible.

But Good Friday, why call it that? How could a man's pain, even if he was the Son of God, save the world? Sloman knew about pain. He had personal experience of it. Like the man himself he too had been put through his agonies. He'd endured and in doing so, had joined the club, become a member of the association, the society, the order of those who suffer.

He poked at the window indicating another warning sign to his neighbour. Red for danger, black for death.

– All over the place this MOD business, he said.

– . . .

– I just tell myself there's no sense in worrying.

– . . .

– See, I've got my heart to think about.

The bloke glanced up momentarily from his magazine.

– Good, is it? said Sloman.

– Something to read, that's all, said the bloke. Are you wanting a look when I've finished?

– No no. No my cup of tea that sort of thing, no thank you. Westerns. That's more my style. A rattling good yarn and a bit description of them desert sunsets.

– . . .

– Bathed in the blood-red glow of the dying sun.

– ?

– *White Feather*, said Sloman. One of the best. I can recommend it.

When the train left the Gareloch behind Sloman felt a rush of relief. For the first time in all his years taking this journey, the deep dark water had bothered him. He imagined it buzzing with blunt-nosed missiles. The big fish. His heart knocked against his chest. All round they must be testing, testing.

He put two fingers to his wrist and counted. Too fast. Way way too fast. He tried the deep breathing. He tried the relaxation. Every day he was laid up in the hospital the physio had put him through his paces. But he'd never got to grips with it. One muscle at a time, she'd chant, bounding round the bed in her white tracksuit, ruining his concentration. When you're under the weather, he thought, a well person can make you feel that much worse. By comparison.

– Spring's late this year.

– . . .

– Last year was the same I'm told. No green showing at Easter. Nothing on the trees till June.

– . . .

– Missed it all myself. Spring, that is, seeing as I was out of action. Due to the heart letting me down.

– . . .

At Crianlarich a few passengers got out but the family opposite showed no signs of being about to remove themselves. The baby had worn itself into an exhausted frazzle from bouncing up and down on the seat. The parents were beginning to quarrel over whose turn it was to pick up the junk it tossed around. There was no end to the activity from that corner.

Sloman was beginning to feel warm, not just comfortable but choked, stifled by the heat. A stream of hot stale air was blowing into his face from a radiator on the wall. He thought about removing his jumper but instead slid open the window. He dragged a hanky over his throat, up around his ears, across his forehead. The train pulled into a station.

– Taynuilt, said Sloman.

– Taynuilt, said the bloke.

– Taynuilt, said the baby's mother.

– Not far now, said Sloman.

Two more stops then off to the Bayview for the bed and the hearty breakfast. Would the proprietress – a stout woman with bad legs – would she see a change in him? Would she detect that beneath the bold red jumper was a damaged heart? It wasn't like a bad leg after all. That kind of injury sticks out for all to see. Every blinking body on the street gawks. But the heart, that was more of a private business. An injury to the heart could quite easily go unnoticed.

The bloke opposite folded his magazine into a wad and put it back in his pocket. Sloman sat back in his chair, stretched his legs. Maybe now they'd have a bit more of a chat.

– I'm wondering how my heart will bear up to the holiday, he said.

– . . .

– You know, you can't take your heart for granted. Not after an attack.

– ?

– A coronary attack! It was touch and go whether I'd last the night. Touch and go!

Come on, Sloman was thinking, say something. Give us a bit of response. What kind of company are you? Somebody tells you they're no a hundred percent, far from it. Somebody tells you, confides in you that their most vital organ has taken a hammering, you don't just sit there, you say something. You respond. Sympathise. Make some crack even.

– You know something, you're no much of a conversationalist. You must be the solitary sort.

– . . .

– Prefer your own company, is that it? I always say there's something not right about being too solitary, too aloof.

– . . .

– I mean we've got to work together and all that. By the way, I don't remember you saying what line you were in.

– Flowers, said the bloke.

– Nice.

– Bouquets and wreaths. More money in wreaths, said the bloke.

– Is that right? said Sloman, and left it at that.

Sloman gasped when he stepped on to the platform. The station was in ruins. All that remained was the clock tower and one wall sagging like an abandoned fort. He could picture a battle scene, the bodies flying off horses, the dust swirling. But the reality was dismal. He'd always admired the station. Not only that but it was a landmark, a milestone on his journey.

The tower was cordoned off with rope and red plastic stickers. A mechanical arm was dismantling the clock-face. Sloman padded over to the centre of activity.

– Didn't see anything about this in the papers, he said. What happened?

– Fire, said a bloke with a camera. He crouched down to get a better angle on the tower.

– But to pull it down! This particular station was a fine building. Victorian, I understand. I mean that's history they're demolishing.

– It's a write-off. You can see for yourself.

The photographer shifted his position and aimed his camera close up at a small area of the debris. Sloman peered at the spot. Under some criss-crossed planks he could just see the tiny arms of a doll jutting out, as if the toy were trying to climb out from under the wreckage.

– I see, I see, said Sloman, moving off.

There was a nip in the air. A brisk breeze was coming off the water and what with the heat in the carriage earlier, Sloman now felt chilled. He laid his case on a bench, snapped it open and removed the Aran cardigan. It spoiled his outfit but there was his health to consider. He buttoned up the cardigan, covering the red jumper bit by bit. When he'd done, only the V at the throat was visible. He lugged his case along the prom to the Bayview, where he discovered that it was the proprietress' day off and the girl in charge didn't even offer to carry his case up the stairs.

He spent the evening as usual – a stroll on the prom, a meal, a drink, another stroll etc., noting the changes, taking care to choose his food and drink sensibly, taking care not to overdo anything, saving himself for the island.

He had forgotten how steep the incline was from the pier to the cliff walk. He was obliged to stop frequently due to breathlessness and the angry thumping in his chest. Violence from the inside was more fearsome than the external variety. You had no defence against your own body, that was the worst of it. Your body was the real enemy. Never mind the muggers, the missiles, the contamination of lochs and rivers, never mind all that. Number one was a force to be reckoned with.

The path had become overgrown since he had last walked along it and, as there was a sheer drop on one side, he inched forward. He didn't notice the dead gull until he was almost upon it and in his hurry to dodge what was left of the bird – a mash of bones and blood-streaked feathers, he almost lost his footing.

It is sunset. Charlie Sloman stands on a rock. His new shoes are splashed by spray flying this way and that. The lion on his chest dances a slow jig as he takes deep breaths of health-giving sea air. Behind him a tree bends back towards the land, its short stiff branches all to one side. It reminds him of his hearth brush, of home.

He is alone with his view. On this part of the shore the grass is tough and sparse, the rocks pitted, black. But where the spray strikes there's a red tinge to the stone, a deep dark red. He watches the sun sink, flatten out and – without any of the anticipated drama – disappear. He puts two fingers to his wrist and counts.

TWILIGHT

THE CHILDREN HAVE MANY NAMES FOR me. *Twilight* is the one I like best. They call me this because, if they see me at all, it is at the time when all the colour goes out of the day, as if it were sucked away by the fierce dragging tide we have on this part of the coast. I say we, but I am not from around here, although I have come to regard it as my home.

At dusk I fetch water from the well at the end of the street, at the time when the flying foxes begin to cross the sky. Just before the streetlights go on – but we do not have so many – these large bats pass over the big banyan tree in the town square. I say town but really it is only a village with a little bit extra, for example the prison. The prison stands on a cliff not far from the house where I live, the house which has become for me both prison and sanctuary.

With little else to do now that the boats have been pulled out of the water, now that the unsold papaya and plantain in the market, the ladies' finger and the chilli have been packed up, now that the crows have stopped arguing in the tree-tops, the street vendors raise their heads to watch the slow heavy procession. I can see only the white of an eye or the glint of a gold tooth as one dark face after another tilts skywards.

The bats fly in a loose, straggling line, like the chain gang which has been laying stones on the road outside my house, the new road which, I've heard say, will bring money and work and visitors. Since I have been here I have had no visitors.

The bats are my timepiece. When I see them, I prepare to go out. There is something sad, something sombre about these unpopular creatures opening and closing their black umbrella wings as if they can't decide on the weather. Small boys like to scare them. Bored from playing around their mothers' heels in the market, they whoop and race on to the new football pitch, armed with pebbles which they hurl into the sky.

Like the bats, I too hunt for food at night. I too have my regular route. I used to take my time, to please myself where I wandered when the day's activities had died down to a murmur, when the marketplace was dark and empty, when only the temple and the toddy-shops were receiving visitors. I do not spend so long on the streets now. Now I am more careful.

There are a few good people who leave out a dish of rice for me. And sometimes chicken scraps. And sometimes buffalo curd. On good nights I might find more food than I can eat before the ants carry it off. Other times nothing but stones and abuse are flung my way. There is no pattern to generosity. In my home town, though, after everything changed for me, things were much worse. I did not go out at all.

My sister still writes once a week with news, for example my mother's eye trouble, for example my father's work problems. My mother's vision is clouding over. My father's work makes him bad-tempered and gives him an excuse to spend too much time drinking arak and feeling sorry for himself. His problems never change. Always it is the glazes. All his life he has tried to perfect a special glaze for his waterpots. When I was little he told me he wanted the glaze to shine like my skin. He does not say this nowadays.

I have not seen my family for several years. Really, I don't think I will see any of them again. My mother is now too old to put up with the discomfort of a long bus journey. This year my sister has learned to drive and the family could come all together by car. But there is always some excuse, for example a doctor's appointment for my mother – which of course she will not keep, for example a rush order for waterpots. My sister does not like to wound me with the truth that really no one wants to come, really no one wants to remember me. To my family I have become a shameful memory.

When I was a child my parents were so proud of me. I was not too dark – the rich bronze my father tried to conjure from his pastes and powders – not too skinny, and had good teeth in spite of the bad well-water. Really it was not hard for my mother to find me a husband when the time came. I did not like the man she chose for me so much, but I accepted him. It was the right thing to do. And before everything began to go wrong with me, he was not so bad really.

Of all people my mother, I hoped, would have had some sympathy, some understanding. But I was no longer the daughter she knew. I had become an unwelcome stranger in my birthplace. My face she no longer recognised as the one from which she had wiped food and dirt and tears a thousand times. In my new skin she feared me. Even in farewell she could not bring herself to embrace me. I had become untouchable, worse than a leper.

Of course my mother had been against the injection from the start. She had always been wary of new ideas, especially anything to do with doctors. Doctors, she said, worked for the government and only cured what it wanted cured. She'd say, when anyone was listening, So why else do they not cure the water we have to drink? And why is the water on Queen Street not bad like ours? I tell you why . . . and so on. My mother believes what she wants to believe.

According to my sister, my mother could have had her vision cleared years ago. The mist which makes her fall down the temple steps, scald herself on the rice water, it could have been altogether removed. But again and again she has put off the operation. Look what happened to Sumona, she says and stumbles on to the verandah. The doctor tells her – he has to shout from the gate as she will no longer let him into the yard – that she spends too much time in bright light. He tells her it is not the well-water but the midday sun which is destroying her sight. So you want me to sit in the dark, as if I'm already in my grave? she says and continues to sit on the veranda from noon until four.

My eyes do not like the sun anymore. I don't see it much and, when I do, it dazzles me. So my mother and I are becoming alike, she blinding herself with too much sunlight, I with too little. But in the dark I see well. There are so many shades of night, now that I have learned them. Darkness is soothing. It is kind. Really I don't understand why people are afraid of the dark, why lights must be kept burning through the night as if darkness itself were evil. It hides. It protects. Its coolness comforts. Darkness is a friend.

A friend only to crooks and devils, my mother would say. And maybe she is right. Indeed the prisoners understand about darkness as well as I. From first light until sunset, gangs are sent out to work on the road. All day in the bright light and heat is plenty punishment without hard labour as well. When I hear the axes begin to ring on the stones – I am usually falling asleep at this time – I feel almost lucky to be resting in bed, alone, safe.

My mother was a friend to me before it happened. Like many women her age, she was eager for grandchildren. Two daughters and a son married by then, but being the eldest, I should have led the way. The two lost babies didn't count. I wasn't trying hard enough, she believed, even though I was so sick my aunt had to be called in to nurse me, even though the doctor explained to the whole family – he came at dinner to make sure no one wandered off before he had finished – that it wasn't wise, actually it was dangerous for me, that the injection was a new way to make me well again. My mother turned the doctor out of the house.

Sura, my husband, who turned out to be less decent than my mother imagined – he spent even more time in toddy-shops than my father – didn't like me to be sick all the time. It was expensive and my aunt's cooking gave him bellyache. He agreed with the doctor. Later, though, he denied this. I hear from my sister that he has changed his ways since becoming husband to my old school-friend and father to two boys.

Such a long time I have been here and still I am angry. With my mother. My husband. My doctor. Myself. Each evening I meet my reflection in the water I draw from the well. Once a day I must see myself as others see me. Once a day is too often.

Rage flares in me as I creep about the streets. It is no wonder the villagers think me mad as well as ugly, a creature who lives by night, sun blind. If I were a child, perhaps I too would hide in doorways, waiting for the freak to come by, sharpening sticks and practising insults. And if I were a mother – but that will never be – maybe I too would cover my baby's eyes as the madwoman passed. As a man stumbling home, my head fuddled from liquor, I too might find it amusing to taunt an unloved creature with dirty propositions. These people I can forgive. But not my family. No, not my family. Not even my sister who writes with news. Not yet. A long time but still too soon. And myself. Can I ever forgive myself?

I can be no one else but me. Really I am the same as I always was. Only the surface has changed, not I, Sumona, whose skin has lost its colour like the sky does at twilight.

Twilight is the name I like best. It does not hurt like some names, for example *Pigmeat*. That hurts because it is true and nothing can be done. My skin lost all its colour after the doctor's injection: now it is like pork, greyish-white, dead-looking. It does not belong in the living world, my skin. Only in a twilight world of shadows, drawn blinds, a world of crooks and devils, as my mother would say.

Tonight I will not rage and burn myself out like the bat who traps itself on the overhead cables and fries to death. Tonight in my silent house, I will no longer be alone. I am to receive a visitor. This morning, as I was about to sleep, I was sent a message. The message was in code – but I could understand it: it was meant for me. Tapped out by an axe, a regular beat, like temple music, ringing against the stone. I got up from my bed and looked out. A line of men, chained at the ankles, bent into their work.

He was looking up so I knew it was he. He could not speak, of course, he could not even show that he had seen me. A prisoner must be humble or he will be beaten to make him so. My father taught us that. Lower your eyes and avoid a beating.

All day I have lain awake, listening to his message as the gang move inch by inch along the road. I have spied on him through the blind from time to time. A tall man, strong, dark. He hits the rocks hard. Tonight I know he is going to escape. He has told me, in his way, what is going to happen. I will be ready for him. I will shelter him in my unlit house and in the darkness he and I will be like any other lovers. I do not know anything about this man. Perhaps he is a killer. But I will welcome him.

THE PRICE OF TEA

I DON'T REALLY REMEMBER MY PATERNAL grand-parents, except that when they visited, the best china was brought out, and the children, my brother and I, were expected to be seen and not heard.

I was in the process of moving house, at the tedious stage of packing box after box of kitchenware and had reached the cutlery drawer, an offputting clutter of implements. Amongst these I discovered an old spoon which I had not noticed for years, a silver teaspoon my grandmother had given me when I was born. My mother, when I was old enough to understand, explained what it meant to be born with a silver spoon in one's mouth. I stored this piece of information, like a collector's-piece alongside all the other odd adult phrases which required explanation, the superstitions, the euphemisms, the exemplary tales, the proverbs.

In fiction, as in life, heirlooms and their poor cousins, hand-me-downs, have their uses. Not only do they provide a tangible link with the hazy past but they become invested with an almost dangerous level of emotional resonance. History, whether we like it or not, presses itself upon us like an uninvited guest when we find great-aunt Lizzie's vase at the back of a cupboard. And if the vase is accidentally smashed or grandfather's watch stops ticking, we feel deprived of, not so much the object, but a whole series of memories relating to the original owner. Heirlooms, then, rapidly develop a fierce hold over their inheritors. Each piece has its own story and if the piece is lost or broken, so, often, is the story.

I have found the spoon.

Here is the story of the spoon.

When the Japanese came, my grandfather, a tall heavy man, was on the verandah, seated in the shade of a banana palm, discussing the plantation accounts with his native under-manager. Inside the airy bungalow my grandmother, a petite and pampered woman who looked younger than her fifty years, was taking tea and writing a letter to her sister in Scotland. In the letter she quizzed her sister about her children's progress at school. Though she saw them – two boys and a girl – only once every two years, she was intent that they stuck in at their lessons and gave value for money. The letter was never finished, never sent.

Why were my grandparents still in residence when the Japanese were steamrolling across Java and thousands of refugees had already flooded into the ports on the north coast? It is possible that they hadn't heard any recent news. The tea plantation was some distance from the southern coast, in the hills north of Bandung. It is also possible that they had assumed, being civilians, that the Geneva convention would be upheld, that they would be ignored. Perhaps they had simply refused to believe the facts, or even sensibly avoided the already chaotic ports, hoping that order would at some point resume. Whatever the reason, life as they had known and mostly enjoyed it up to that point, instantly ceased.

Without any preliminaries, grandfather was ordered into one of two armed trucks, and driven away, leaving grandmother vainly attempting to rally the servants, most of whom had already fled into the jungle. Those who remained had fallen on their knees in front of the Japanese and were begging for mercy. This was quite understandable. However frightening it might have been to be hustled into the back of a truck, it was much worse to be tied to a tree and shot, which was what they must have expected. In fact this only happened to one of them, a cook, caught in the act of stealing some of grandmother's jewellery. After the unfortunate man had been dealt with and before the soldiers sacked and burnt the house, the commanding officer returned the stolen goods to grandmother. He also gave her a canvas bag, and instructed her to fill it, speedo.

It was not a large bag but she managed to squeeze in, along with toiletries and a few articles of clothing – at which the soldiers laughed long and hard – some jewellery and some small items of silverware. It didn't occur to her that she was being taken prisoner, which perhaps explains her choice of a lace blouse and white silk hat. She intended to wear her best on the boat on which she and her husband would, most certainly, be sent home.

It was five years before such a boat materialised and the intervening years were such that, when she remembered herself on that day – choosing between the peach silk and the tussore – it was with utter derision. Arriving at the

POW camp wearing a silk hat and a pair of kid gloves, a crocodile handbag hanging on her arm. Requesting to use the Rest Room to freshen up as the dust from the truck had soiled her outfit. When she was shown the latrines, she fainted.

Of the two, grandmother was the luckier. The coastal camp to which she had been taken was a work camp. Being accustomed to a life of privilege, in which she was expected to do no physical work other than a little light gardening, she did not take easily to road mending around the camp. The simple equation of no work, no food was, however, a most effective form of persuasion. Even in return for back-breaking toil, rations were scandalously small; yet considerably more than what grandfather was given.

He was imprisoned some distance from the coast in an area of jungle swamp. There was little use to which the Japanese could put these prisoners and, so, having no value to their captors, they were consistently starved. Like so many, grandfather's health was destroyed by the effects of malaria, malnutrition, dysentery, beriberi. On more than one occasion he was left for dead. How did he survive? He was not a young man, knew nothing of his wife's fate, indeed was convinced, on many an occasion – as was she – that the other was dead. He went in weighing sixteen stone and came out weighing eight. These are all the facts I have.

Grandmother didn't take long to realise how foolish she had been in taking up space in that small bag with anything other than what she could trade. Though prisoners were fed the same rice and broth day after day, year after year, other foodstuffs could be obtained, at a price. For the first time in her life, grandmother was truly wealthy: stitched into her skirt for safe-keeping, she had some silver.

Though conditions were very tough at the women's camp, the warders' greatest crime was neglect. Though there was little active ill-treatment of prisoners, there was little assistance. Medication was supplied at the whim of the commanding officer and sick leave was rarely permitted. The dormitories were disease-ridden and overcrowded. A bed was a bamboo platform the size of a coffin. Babies were born here to mothers who couldn't feed them and no milk was provided. It was of no importance to the Japanese that a child survive, but for the prisoners a child was hope, of a chance, of a future.

In grandmother's dormitory were several younger women who were pregnant when they were taken prisoner. One of these was Lotte, whose bunk lay next to grandmother's. Her husband had been a farmer on Java. Unlike grandmother, Lotte was a robust, independent woman. She had always taken part in the work of the farm whereas grandmother's involvement in the tea plantation had been no more than to query accounts and organise the household. The two women had nothing in common. Grandmother hated the total lack of privacy in the camp and would go to great lengths to maintain shreds of personal modesty. Lotte, on the other hand, would shamelessly strip off her rags and show the entire dormitory her swollen belly.

Nothing in common, yet, lying at night on the bunks, trying to sleep, when it got even hotter and bruised bodies hurt even more, Lotte would talk and grandmother would listen. Though prisoners quickly learnt that trust was dangerous, everyone took the risk at times, which is how

176

grandmother knew that, unlike her, Lotte had next to nothing sewn into her skirt.

Even with her bits of silver, how did grandmother survive? She was so unfit for any kind of hardship that the road work alone could have killed her.

When Lotte's baby girl was born she was, like most babies born in the camp, pitifully underweight, always hungry even after a feed, and wasn't putting on weight. The slightest infection could have killed her. Lotte herself was sinking into an exhausted stupor.

One night when she knew the traders were at the fence, grandmother had words with them. They shook their heads at her request, offered instead energy-giving yeast – which she must have found so hard to resist – but she was insistent, milk or nothing. The baby cried all night and so did Lotte. The following evening the traders returned, with a can of powdered milk and grandmother handed over all but one of her six silver teaspoons. The last she slipped into the can, for the baby.

What made her do this? Camp conditions made this kind of sacrifice seem more of an act of madness than anything else. She had not been, from what I could discover, a particularly generous person previous to the camp, never having felt she could quite afford generosity. Nor was she sentimental about children, at least not her own, with whom she had a formal, distant relationship. Lotte had not asked for help, though she obviously needed it. And not just milk, but a spoon, silver, which might save her own life later. Had superstition got a grip on her?

Though the baby died from a virus a few weeks later, Lotte didn't forget the gift and, when she had regained a fraction of her original strength, she more than repaid the kindness. She and grandmother worked as a team on the roads, transporting cut rocks from a lorry, one by one, and laying them. Grandmother had injured her back early on and suffered intensely from the continual bending and when eventually released, spent her first year of freedom encased in plaster. Had it not been for Lotte, she would have been crippled, at least. Each prisoner had a quota of work to perform for the daily rice and gruel and it was a punishable offence to do another's work for them. Yet, whenever the guards were a safe distance away, Lotte laid half of grandmother's stones as well as her own.

When peace came to the island, evacuation of the camps was slow as many of the prisoners, like grandmother, were too weak to walk. As she was being carried out on a stretcher, Lotte limped over and pressed a small parcel into her hand. It contained the spoon and a note which read: for the baby. The two women didn't meet again.

Some months later, in a hospital in Darwin, British POWs were being reunited. What happened when grandfather met grandmother? What did they notice when they first saw each other? What did they say? How did they greet each other? Did being together again give them a charge of energy? Did they immediately begin chattering, anxious to catch up on those lost years, or did they sit in silence, holding hands, simply glad to be together again, alive?

I don't have answers to these questions, the ones we naturally ask to help us picture a scene. I can't colour in this picture, I can't provide the atmosphere for an emotional or calm meeting between them because all I know is that when they met, they did not recognise each other. Grandfather, skeletal, recovering from one of the malarial fevers which were to haunt him all his life, demanded that the crazy old woman be taken away. Grandmother had to identify herself to him by her wedding-ring and the last of the family silver, a teaspoon.

What kind of future was there for two people who, though married for twenty-five years, now saw each other as strangers? Two people who had been changed beyond recognition? Having seen in their separate camps the collapse of all standards of human behaviour what would each not imagine the other had been party to? Two people who had previously dressed for dinner seven nights a week and conversed about rhododendrons in the driveway or the price of tea, how would they begin? Which questions would they ask, which would they avoid? Would they speak only of the future, make plans? Did one ever ask the other, What did they do to you? Or the even harder question, What did you do to others? Eat human flesh? And worse, cheat, betray, murder? How did they piece together any kind of life?

Sitting, years later, in the quiet English village they retired to, looking through the English drizzle at the soft green meadow rolling down to the dovecot and the slowly turning millwheel, did one ever dare to ask the other that dreaded question: what's on your mind?

I did not know my paternal grandparents. They did not know each other. I did not know Lotte, or her baby, but I carry their stories with me and when the time comes, will pass them on.

TESS GALLAGHER

The Lover Of Horses

'Lilting and powerful stories . . . these tales of uncelebrated people who live in small American towns and humdrum suburbs are superb in their deft analysis of the shifting sands on which our emotional lives are built'
Sunday Times

'A wonderful short story collection. Tess Gallagher has a poet's passion for language and a keen eye for detail'   Caryl Phillips

'The characters in *The Lover of Horses* are redolent of a great tradition in American literature, and specifically of Raymond Carver's writing: the minstrels in the suburbs who are their own instruments. In this collection they have all learnt to play Gallagher's Music'
Literary Review

'A fine story-writer . . . wonderful stories'
Guardian

MOY McCRORY

Bleeding Sinners

'*Bleeding Sinners* deals with women's fertility; its pain and pleasure; its consequences in a world fettered by ignorance and fear. Its eleven short stories range from the frankly fantastic – as when a bored wife wakes up to find her husband has turned into a giant sprouting potato – to the naturalistic Belfast setting of the title piece . . . This is an extraordinary book about ordinary experience, beautifully written and observed'   *Time Out*

'Moy McCrory has a laser-sharp eye and knife-like pen . . . the story "Drop Stars Fall in Unmarked Places" is a consciously literary poetic gem . . . by itself it makes *Bleeding Sinners* worth the price and marks Moy McCrory as a writer to watch'
Scotland on Sunday

'Her prose style is taut and muscular, her narrative skill tackles complex interwoven time-scapes with deceptive ease . . . this is a book which demands to be read'   *Spare Rib*

A Selected List of Titles Available from Minerva

While every effort is made to keep prices low, it is sometimes necessary to increase prices at short notice. Mandarin Paperbacks reserves the right to show new retail prices on covers which may differ from those previously advertised in the text or elsewhere.

The prices shown below were correct at the time of going to press.

Fiction

☐ 7493 9026 3	**I Pass Like Night**	Jonathan Ames	£3.99 BX
☐ 7493 9006 9	**The Tidewater Tales**	John Bath	£4.99 BX
☐ 7493 9004 2	**A Casual Brutality**	Neil Blessondath	£4.50 BX
☐ 7493 9028 2	**Interior**	Justin Cartwright	£3.99 BC
☐ 7493 9002 6	**No Telephone to Heaven**	Michelle Cliff	£3.99 BX
☐ 7493 9028 X	**Not Not While the Giro**	James Kelman	£4.50 BX
☐ 7493 9011 5	**Parable of the Blind**	Gert Hofmann	£3.99 BC
☐ 7493 9010 7	**The Inventor**	Jakov Lind	£3.99 BC
☐ 7493 9003 4	**Fall of the Imam**	Nawal El Saadewi	£3.99 BC

Non-Fiction

☐ 7493 9012 3	**Days in the Life**	Jonathon Green	£4.99 BC
☐ 7493 9019 0	**In Search of J D Salinger**	Ian Hamilton	£4.99 BX
☐ 7493 9023 9	**Stealing from a Deep Place**	Brian Hall	£3.99 BX
☐ 7493 9005 0	**The Orton Diaries**	John Lahr	£5.99 BC
☐ 7493 9014 X	**Nora**	Brenda Maddox	£6.99 BC

All these books are available at your bookshop or newsagent, or can be ordered direct from the publisher. Just tick the titles you want and fill in the form below. Available in:
BX: British Commonwealth excluding Canada
BC: British Commonwealth including Canada

Mandarin Paperbacks, Cash Sales Department, PO Box 11, Falmouth, Cornwall TR10 9EN.

Please send cheque or postal order, no currency, for purchase price quoted and allow the following for postage and packing:

UK	80p for the first book, 20p for each additional book ordered to a maximum charge of £2.00.
BFPO	80p for the first book, 20p for each additional book.
Overseas including Eire	£1.50 for the first book, £1.00 for the second and 30p for each additional book thereafter.

NAME (Block letters) ....

ADDRESS ....

....

....